Walking Words

for a great
walking partner
love,
John

Also by Eduardo Galeano

Walking Words

Eduardo Galeano

with woodcuts by
José Francisco Borges

translated by
Mark Fried

W · W · Norton & Company
New York   London

First published as a Norton paperback 1997

Portions of this material have appeared in *Cojunctions* and *Mother Jones*.

The text of this book is composed in Garamond No. 3 with the display set in
Bogeda Serif Medium
Composition and manufacturing by The Maple-Vail Book Manufacturing Group.
Book Design by Margaret M. Wagner

L.C. no. 95-195317

ISBN 0-393-03782-7
ISBN 0-393-31514-2 pbk.

W. W. Norton & Company, Inc., 500 Fifth Avenue, New York, N.Y. 10110
W. W. Norton & Company Ltd., 10 Coptic Street, London WC1A 1PU

1 2 3 4 5 6 7 8 9 0

to Helena Villagra

Viewed up close, nobody is normal.

Caetano Veloso

Contents

The author wishes to acknowledge the suggestions
of Pepe Barrientos, Susana Iglesias, Iván Kmaid,
Mariana Mactas, Eric Nepomuceno, Mercedes Ramírez,
and Chola Riccetto, who were patient enough to
read the original draft.

Walking Words

Window on This Book

A makeshift table, some movable type made of lead or wood, a press that might have been Gutenberg's: the workshop of José Francisco Borges in the town of Bezerros, in the hinterlands of Brazil's Northeast.

The air smells of ink and wood. Planks are piled high waiting for Borges's knife, and prints fresh off the woodcuts hang on wires to dry. Borges looks at me, his face like carved wood, and doesn't say a word.

In the TV era, Borges remains an artist of the old *cordel* tradition. In tiny booklets, he recounts events and legends: he writes the verses, carves the woodcuts, prints them, carries them from town to town on his back, and offers them for sale in marketplaces where he sings the feats of men and ghosts.

I have come to his workshop to propose a joint project. I venture my idea: his illustrations, his woodcuts, and my words. He is silent. I talk on, explaining. And he says nothing.

On it goes for quite a while, until suddenly I realize that my words have no music. I'm blowing through a broken flute. The unborn can't be explained or understood: you feel it, you touch it when it moves. So I stop explaining and I tell him the stories. I tell him the stories of ghouls and fools that I'd like to write, voices I've collected in my dreamlike wanderings or heard in my wakeful dreams, realities made delirious, deliria made real.

I tell him the stories, and this book is born.

Story of the Seven Prodigies

From the mouth of the Amazon to All Saints Bay, never was there a woman so difficult or a man so magical.

To win María's favor, José performed seven wonders.

María's father said: "He's nothing but skin and bones."

So José spread in the air a lace tablecloth no hand had fashioned, and commanded: "Table, set thyself."

And a banquet of many steaming dishes was served by no one on the floating cloth. And it was a joy for every palate.

But María ate not so much as a grain of rice.

The richest man in town, lord of land and people, declared: "He's a penniless piece of shit."

So José called to his goat, which gamboled over from nowhere, and commanded: "Shit goat."

And the goat shat gold. And there was gold for every palm.

But María turned her back on the brilliance.

María's boyfriend, who was a fisherman, said: "He knows nothing about fishing."

So José stood at the edge of the sea and blew. He blew with lungs that were not his own, and he commanded: "Sea, dry thyself."

And the sea withdrew, leaving the sand silvery with fish. And the fish filled everyone's baskets to overflowing.

But María held her nose.

María's dead husband, a phantom of fire, said: "I'll turn him into charcoal."

And flames attacked José on all sides.

So José commanded, with a voice that was not his own: "Fire, refresh me."

And he bathed himself in the blaze. And everyone's eyes leapt out of their sockets.

But María shut her eyelids.

The town priest declared: "He ought to be in hell."

And he pronounced José guilty of witchcraft and of making a pact with the Devil.

So José grabbed the priest by the scruff of the neck and commanded: "Arm, stretch thyself."

And José's arm, which was no longer his own, picked up the priest

and lowered him into the fiery depths of hell. And everyone's jaw dropped.

But María cried out in horror. And in a twinkling that enormous arm returned the singed priest.

The policeman said: "He ought to be in jail."

And he leapt at José, truncheon in hand.

So José commanded: "Stick, hit."

And the truncheon beat the policeman, who ran off pursued by his own weapon and was lost from sight. And everyone laughed. María too.

And María offered José a sprig of coriander and a white rose.

The judge declared: "He ought to be killed."

And José was convicted of contempt, violation of the right of property (the father's over his daughter and the dead man's over his widow), disturbing the peace, assault on an officer, and attempted priesticide.

The executioner raised his ax over José's neck as he lay bound hand and foot.

So José commanded: "Neck, resist."

And the ax fell, and his neck shattered it.

It was time for a feast. And everyone celebrated the humiliation of human law and the defeat of laws divine.

María, still wet with tears, offered José a piece of cheese and a red rose.

And José, naked champion, conquered conqueror, trembled at the knees.

Window on the Word (I)

Storytellers, storysingers, only spin their tales while the snow falls. That's the way it's done. The Indians of North America are very careful about this matter of stories. They say that while stories are being told, plants don't pay attention to growing and birds forget to feed their young.

Story of the Female Avenger and the Archangel in the Palace of Sinners

Dear Mr. Writer:

I am moved to write to you not out of admiration but out of pity for your minimal inspiration and limited imagination. In your prose, which is as proper as it is pedestrian, readers never find anything they haven't already read.

This letter offers you the chance to reveal your normally hidden talent, that is, if you have some hidden somewhere. Believe me, you don't need to be a genius to cook up a good story with all the ingredients I'll give you. You may be wondering: Why me and not another? In the first place, someone gave me your address. In the second place, all writers worth their salt are six feet under where the postman doesn't go.

Let's start with the scene: high on a hill, in a white tower that reached the stars, stood the brothel of Comayagua. The church was below. Half the town went to the brothel, the whole town went to mass and the processions. That's how Comayagua yawned its way through history.

In case it's of any use, I'll transcribe a traveler's summation of the attitude of the respectable ladies: *The scandal began here after Independence when close dances hit town. In the times of the Spaniards, people danced apart without touching, the minuet from France, the jota from Aragón. . .*

The brothel belonged to Don Idilio Gallo. The girls worked night and day without a moment's rest. Don Idilio drained their youth to the last drop. When they were bone-dry, he sent them back to the street. I beg you not to spend too many words on this point, dear writer, given your notorious tendency to preach, and do allow Calamity Jane to come on stage right away. After all, while their treatment may have left something to be desired, Don Idilio Gallo's girls didn't have it so bad—compared with the rest of the frogs croaking at the bottom of that hole.

Calamity Jane arrived in bad shape, slumped over the back of her horse Satan. She came from the Far West, chased by the echoes of Apache drums. She crossed the mountains of three countries, guided by the reflections of her diamond ring on rocky canyon walls. Calamity brought along the ring, which disappeared the first night. And she also brought along her well-earned fame of having a mother's heart, a happy trigger finger, an infallible lasso, and marked cards.

The girls took her in without Don Idilio knowing. She slept for a week. When she awoke, she faced him: "The hat," she said.

Instead of uncovering his head, Don Idilio, who wasn't much of a gentleman, pulled his Stetson down to his eyebrows. Calamity drew her Colt and blew it off with one shot.

Continuing to shoot, she kept the hat in the air. When the hat-turned-colander finally came down, Don Idilio Gallo let out a moan and Calamity blew the smoke from her gun. "That's why I didn't stay in Rapid City," she said. "They kill a lot in that shit hole."

Does mentioning the names Colt or Stetson seem superfluous? I'm not surprised. But a professional writer ought to know that in a credible narrative the smallest details matter most. And by the way, I suggest you take into account that Calamity used a Springfield rifle, not a Winchester as some idiots claim.

Let's continue. They played poker. The bets went up as the bottles of Jamaican rum went down, until Don Idilio lost the brothel and everything else. That overbearing pitiless man didn't even blink. He accepted his ruin with the fatalism characteristic of the Gallos, descendants of sentries who in earthquakes would sit and wait for the house to fall in on them. Calamity gave him a letter of recommendation for Buffalo Bill's circus. With nothing else in his pockets, Don Idilio left for Paris. There he put on feathers and dressed up as a redskin chief, posed for profile shots, and died of pneumonia.

The brothel, which had been cold as a hospital and hard as a barracks, became filled up with birds and guitars, plants and colors. From dusk till dawn the girls opened their legs. But during the day, and until the first bells of the Angelus, they opened their ears. Experience gave them the idea. They knew that behind every macho with balls hides a shipwrecked sailor begging for refuge. Their confessional was so successful that it overflowed with multitudes from the enemy city of Tegucigalpa and from everywhere else. On the sides of the hill, long lines of men waited their turn to pour out doubts and secrets and hidden fears, dreams and nightmares. The church couldn't compete. Priests, as you know, only hear the confession of sins, which is what people least need to confess.

Meanwhile, Calamity got busy straightening out her papers with Mr. Government. This woman who had always worn pants put on a skirt. She tucked a Collins bayonet into her garter and money into her undershirt.

"In an envelope," instructed Mr. Government when Calamity slipped him a fistful of hot bills. And by decree the brothel, non-profit cooperative that it was, was exempted from all taxes and new whorehouses were prohibited in the entire national territory.

In that year of crazy prosperity, the archangel arrived. According to tradition, the palace of sinners closed its doors every Friday during Lent. And according to tradition, after Jesus of Nazareth had traveled Calvary Street on the shoulders of pious women, and the last echoes of Passion canticles and Via Crucis prayers had faded, a headless horseman would appear at full gallop from the mouth of the night. The horse would kick the brothel doors, give a few terrifying bucks, and tear off, chased by whirlwinds and puffs of sulfur. Then, according to tradition, one of the wayward sheep would repent and tearfully abandon her lustful ways to begin an honest life.

That Friday, the headless horseman galloped in, blind with fury like every year, but this time the doors were open wide. The black horse went right through the brothel and disappeared in the distance; the horseman rolled onto the ground, knocked into a Tiffany lamp, and crashed against a wall. He woke up in a woman's arms. "Listen, señora," he protested.

"Señorita," Calamity Jane corrected him.

The horseman was an archangel, an elderly dwarf with a red nose and the voice of a child, dressed by God to look like a headless devil and frighten licentious women.

There was lightning and rain all night and the world awoke more luminous than ever. Morning surprised the archangel in the midst of a sitz bath, sitting in a pool of green papaya milk. The poor man had hurt his ass when the rope that lowered him from heaven broke. Beside him, Calamity, mouth open, let him do as he pleased. With honey and cinnamon, the archangel cleansed her tongue soiled by insolent cursing.

Please, I beg you, don't offend me by asking if this really happened. I'm offering it to you so you'll make it happen. I'm not asking you to describe the rain falling the night the archangel arrived: I'm demanding that you get me wet. Make up your mind, Mr. Writer, and for once in your life be the flower that smells rather than the chronicler of the aroma. There's not much pleasure in writing what you live. The challenge is to live what you write. And at your age it's time you learned.

I'll continue. As you know from the available iconography, archangels have no sex but they do have stomachs. If Adam fell for a plain old apple, how was the archangel not to give in? The brothel offered him the delicacies of its orchard: the golden flesh of the mango, the dizzying breath of the passion fruit, the freshness of the pineapple, the softness of the guanabana and the avocado.

And, as everyone knows, archangels have souls; and a soul needs to confess, even if it doesn't sin. Calamity complained about the Wild West and the archangel complained about Heaven. Chocolate kept them company by day; rum by night. She said that if she owned Wyoming and hell, she would rent out Wyoming and live in hell. And he said that having spent all eternity serving the Lord in Paradise by doing the hardest chores, the Ingrate thanked him by sending him to earth to redeem drunks and whores. She told rude secrets about General Custer and Sheriff Wild Bill Hickok, and he railed against the advisers of the Holiest One. And talking, they discovered they had spent their entire lives alone and hadn't realized it.

Some afternoons Calamity took the archangel out for a walk in the streets of Comayagua in a baby carriage. They walked proudly, impervious to resentment and envy. They were pursued by the evil tongues of anti-imperialists, atheists, and the advocates of virtue and good manners. And there were always skeptics who would elbow each other and ask under their breath: How come Calamity Jane doesn't understand a word of English? What kind of an archangel doesn't have wings or a sword of fire and doesn't know a word of Latin? How come the two of them talk with accents from around here?

I don't know if this happened. I only know that it deserves to have happened.

The rest is the least of it. Time covered all tracks. You might imagine that the archangel had a fine time, life was a lot more fun than salvation. But you might also suppose that in the end Calamity tired of it all. You could suppose that in a palace wallpapered with mirrors that gave away her age she would find no place to hide. Imagine the brothel in its glory, with the National Symphonic Orchestra playing till dawn, and one night Calamity dances the belly dance, naked under a red negligee, and the audience applauds with cackles and sniggers and she fights back the tears. And the next day she leaves. She leaves without saying goodbye, when no one is looking. Her horse Satan kneels down to help her mount. She doesn't go north, back to her origins. She continues the trip south toward her destiny. Someone must have heard the sound of hoofbeats and the whistle. She was whistling. To keep herself company? To get up her courage? You choose.

And the archangel? Did Calamity take him along in her lap? Did he go back to heaven? Did he try? Did he become a man at last, a new Idilio Gallo? Don't bother asking. No one could answer, not in Comayagua or in any other town on the planet. Sorry, Mr. Writer, *homo scribere,* you have no choice but to make it up.

Yours,

(Signature illegible)

Window on the Word (II)

In Haiti, stories may not be told during the day. Anyone who tells a story before dark is disgraced: the mountain throws a stone at his head, his mother walks on all fours.

Nighttime draws out what is sacred, and those who know how to tell stories know that the name is the very thing that it names.

Window on the Word (III)

In the Guaraní language, *ñe'ē* means both "word" and "soul."

The Guaraní Indians believe that those who lie or squander words betray the soul.

Story of the Lizard Who Had the Habit of Dining on His Wives

At the edge of the river, hidden by tall grass, a woman is reading.

Once upon a time, the book tells, there lived the lord of a vast dominion. Everything belonged to him: the town of Lucanamarca and everything around it, the wild beasts and the branded, the wild people and the tame, everything, the high and the low, the dry and the wet, everything that could remember, everything that could forget.

But the lord had no heir. Each day his wife said a thousand prayers, begging for the blessing of a son, and each night she lit a thousand candles.

God wearied of haughty pleas from a woman who asked for something He didn't want to give. At long last, either out of divine mercy or simply to be rid of her, He performed a miracle. And joy descended on the household.

The child had a human face and the body of a lizard.

In time he learned to speak, but he slithered along on his belly. The finest tutors from Ayacucho taught him to read, but his claws could not write.

When he was eighteen, he asked for a wife.

His wealthy father found him one, and with great pomp the wedding took place in the home of the priest.

The very first night the lizard threw himself on his wife and devoured her. When the sun peeped over the horizon, the nuptial bed held only a sleeping widower surrounded by bones.

Later on, the lizard demanded another wife. And there was another wedding and another devouring. Then the glutton needed yet another. And on it went.

Fiancées were never lacking. In the homes of the poor, there was always an extra girl.

With the waters of the river caressing his belly, Dulcidio takes his siesta.

He opens one eye and there she is. She's reading. Never in his life has he seen a woman wearing glasses.

Dulcidio raises his long snout: "What are you reading?"

She lowers her book, looks at him calmly, and says: "Legends."

"Legends?"

"Old voices."

"What for?"

She shrugs her shoulders: "Company."

This woman doesn't seem to be from the mountains or the jungle or the coast.

"I too know how to read," says Dulcidio.

She closes her book and turns away.

When Dulcidio asks her who she is and where she comes from, the woman disappears.

The following Sunday, when Dulcidio wakes from his siesta, she is there. No book, but wearing glasses.

Seated in the sand, her feet hidden under many colorful skirts, she is really there, she has been there forever. She casts her eye at the intruder lolling around in the sun.

Dulcidio sets things straight. He raises a horny claw and waves it toward the blue mountains on the horizon: "As far as you can see, as far as you can walk. It's all mine."

She doesn't even glance at the vast kingdom, and she remains silent. A very silent silence.

The heir insists. The lambs and the Indians are at his command. He is lord of that whole expanse of land and water and air, and also of the strip of sand on which she sits: "You have my permission," he assures her.

She tosses back her long black braid, like someone who hears rain, and the very saurian fellow points out that he is rich but humble, studious and hardworking, and above all a gentleman who wants to have a family. It's cruel destiny that wants to keep him a widower.

Her head bowed, she reflects on this mystery.

Dulcidio hovers. He whispers: "Can I ask you a favor?"

And he snuggles up to her, and turns his back.

"Scratch my back," he begs, "I can't reach."

She stretches out her hand, caresses the steely scales, and exclaims: "It's like silk."

Dulcidio trembles, closes his eyes, opens his mouth, stiffens his tail, and feels things he has never felt before.

But when he looks around, she's gone.

He rushes full tilt through the grass looking for her, back and forth, in all directions. No trace of her.

The following Sunday, she doesn't come to the riverbank. Or the next Sunday, or the next.

Ever since he first saw her, he sees nothing else.

The sleepyhead no longer sleeps, the glutton no longer eats. Dulcidio's bedroom is no longer the happy sanctuary where he took his rest under the watchful gaze of his late wives. Their photographs still

cover the walls from top to bottom, the heart-shaped frames gar-
landed with orange blossoms. Dulcidio, condemned to solitude, lies
buried under the covers, blanketed by sorrow. Doctors and healers
come from all over, but none can stem the ascent of his fever and the
collapse of everything else.

Clinging to the transistor radio he bought from a passing Turk,
Dulcidio suffers through his nights and days sighing and listening to
melodies long out of fashion. His parents, despairing, watch him
pine away. He no longer demands a wife by declaring: "I'm hungry."
Now he moans: "I am a beggar for love." And with his broken voice
and an alarming bent for rhyme, he mumbles agonized homages to
the lady who stole his nerve and his verve.

All the servants set out to find her. They scour heaven and earth,
but they don't even know the name of the one who vanished, and no
one has ever seen a woman wearing glasses in these valleys or beyond.

One Sunday afternoon, Dulcidio has a premonition. He manages to
get up, barely, and he drags himself uneasily to the riverbank.

And there she is.

Bathed in tears, Dulcidio proclaims his love for this disdainful and
elusive overgrown girl. He confesses, "Of thirst I am dying for your
love like wine," proclaims, "I'll burst from crying oh dove so divine,"
and showers her with other sweet words.

The wedding day arrives. Everyone is delighted for it's been a long time since the last feast, and the only one who gets married here is Dulcidio. He's such a good customer, the priest gives him a discount.

Charango music engulfs the sweethearts, and the harp and the violins sing in all their glory. Everyone drinks to the happy couple's eternal love, and rivers of planter's punch flow under the floral wreaths.

Dulcidio is sporting a new skin, reddish on his back and greenish-blue on his prodigious tail.

When at last the two are alone, and the hour of truth arrives, he proclaims: "I give you my heart, till death do us part."

She blows out the candle in a single breath, lets fall her wedding dress, soft and thick with lace, slowly removes her glasses, and says: "Don't be a jerk. Knock off the bullshit."

With one tug she unsheathes him as if he were a sword. She flings his skin to the floor and embraces his naked body, setting it on fire.

Later, Dulcidio sleeps deeply, curled up against this woman, and for the first time in his life he dreams.

She eats him as he sleeps. She swallows him bit by bit, from the tail to the head, making no noise and not chewing hard, careful not to wake him so that he won't have a bad impression.

Window on Time

In Cajamarca, January is the time to weave.

In February delicate flowers and colored belts appear. The rivers sing and it's carnival time.

In March cows and potatoes give birth.

In April ears of corn grow in silence.

In May the crops are harvested.

In the dry days of June, new land is made ready.

There are weddings and fiestas in July, and devil's thistles come up in the furrows.

August, red sky, is the time of winds and plagues.

The ripe moon, not the green moon, is for planting in September.

October pleads to God to let the rains fall.

In November the dead rule.

In December life celebrates.

Window on Harbingers

Corn leaves lose their vigor,
  of a sudden blackberries flower,
  thrushes sing without a pause,
  hens mate clucking, wings raised,
  frogs hop uphill not down,
  piglets dance,
  snails go into hiding,
  snakes come into view,
  owls appear,
  swallows fly in tight circles,
  vultures fly in a line,
  geese fly up from the sea
  and Mount Pelagatos and Mount Tantarica wear caps of clouds.
  These are the signs of the rainy season in Cajamarca, according to
those who know the whys of the whens.

Story of the Fatal Encounter between the Desert Bandit and the Repentant Poet

He was the survivor.

Firmino, old master in the art of banditry, was fleeing toward the countryside near Pernambuco. In an ambush at the foot of a precipice, army bullets had done in his woman and all his friends. He had been mutilated inside, and his remains wandered sadly in solitude.

That night it rained hard in the desert, something that never happens. Lightning revealed several skeletons dressed in military uniforms and hats, kicking in the air. The victims of many years of outrage had come to collect from Firmino the time he owed them for having dispatched them too soon. And their ghostly howls clamored for vengeance.

Waving his knife and swinging the butt of his rifle, Firmino fought the army of bones that rose up with the storm.

At last the rain stopped, as suddenly as it began. And in a moment, all the moisture evaporated and the dead went back to sleep under the dry ground.

Firmino, greatest scoundrel of the kingdom, could continue his flight.

After a long march, he cut some branches to make a fire and the bushes bled.

Firmino understood. But he pushed on.

The lost will be the found, sang Sabino the poet, and the earth will give birth to stars that will humble the heavens. The dumb will be radio announcers and we will have hospitals without sick people where today we have sick people without hospitals.

Reciter of verses in marketplaces far from the coast, Sabino the poet sang the prophecies of the red cow. The cow, which flew in his dreams, told him that the desert would be sea and fields of stone would burst with verdure, and that those in the know had seen birth without death and weeks full of Sundays.

This he sang until he grew weary. The poet Sabino got sick of reciting and waiting. And he repented having spent his life on a pilgrimage amid the poor and the damned in a hell of stone. He discovered that things are the way they are because they've always been and always will be the way God wants them. And he gave up his nights with the crazy cow that dreamt him rubbish. And he went over to the government. No longer did he raise his wooden sword to vent the serpent of sadness, but to punish the enemies of the established order.

Firmino continued walking toward the countryside of Pernambuco or wherever his legs would carry him.

One morning, not far from some hamlet, footsteps awakened him. He leapt up and pulled out his knife. But when he saw Sabino, a boiled chicken in suit and tie, standing in the middle of the thicket, the bandit calmly started shredding tobacco.

The poet introduced himself: Sabino, humble rhapsode at your service; he said that he had always dreamed of meeting the atrocious scourge of the desert, the lord of evil, and today destiny affords me this surprise which I certainly do not merit and which for me means more, much more than. . .

Firmino rolled a cigarette and lit up.

"A great honor," whispered Sabino, swallowing hard.

A few flies were the only audience.

The bandit sent a few smoke rings skyward, and sized up the stuttering bookworm before blowing him away.

Sabino, his face down, counted ants; but suddenly he drew his sword.

The wooden saber trembled in his hand. His voice shook even more: "I'd like to ask you a little favor," he sighed.

He wiped his forehead and eyes with a handkerchief, and he mouthed his entreaty: "Allow me . . . to cut off your head."

Firmino laughed out loud, a great belly laugh that rolled and rolled until he had used up all the laughter stored away since the last time he laughed so very long ago. Then he coughed.

And then he stretched out his neck: "Proceed, doctor."

The poet Sabino held the wooden sword with both hands and hung on for dear life.

The bandit Firmino stood up and stroked his neck.

The poet blinked. A rabbit-like groan escaped him and at last he was able to plead: "Say no."

The brigand did him the favor. Why not? You don't deny that to anyone. So the terror of the Northeast said: "No."

But the poet muttered: "Say no . . . with your head."

And then, when the bandit shook his head, it came loose and rolled on the ground.

The victory of Civilization over Barbarism made headlines across the front pages of the local, regional, national, continental, and global press. In a public ceremony carried live by the BBC of London, Sabino received the reward and donated it to charity. The book that narrated his feat was translated into English, French, German, and Esperanto, and the poet Sabino was chosen Man of the Year by *Time*.

Firmino's soul went straight to heaven.

On earth his corpse was split in two. The body was thrown to the vultures and the head to the scientists. Before his mummified head landed in a case in the Museum of Cangaceiros, the scientists proved that Firmino had been an ectomorphic-type higher mammal belonging to the Brazilian-Xanthodermic group. Their analysis revealed a psychopathic personality evidenced by certain bulges in the skull characteristic of cold-blooded assassins from the mountains of obscure countries. The subject's criminal destiny was also apparent from one ear that was nine millimeters shorter than the other, and from the pointed head and oversized jaws with large eyeteeth that continued chewing after he was dead.

Firmino went to heaven because that's where his woman was, and because someone had told him there would be room up there for knights-errant fallen in the noble art of warfare.

He was a knight without a horse. He went to heaven on foot, all the way up the high road to glory, with his Winchester as a walking stick and a silver dagger at his waist. A measured gait, elegantly armored. Bathed in perfume, glistening with brilliantine, rings shining on every finger, Firmino wore a large cross of glowing bullets and a Napoleon hat dripping medals and pounds sterling and other trinkets. After a long ascent, he arrived at the gates of Paradise. And Saint Peter would not let him in.

God himself sent word to forbid him entry. The Supreme Being could not close his ears to the unanimous clamor of angels, archangels, and saints. Firmino's woman, who got into heaven by mistake, sleeps with them all. She is the only fire burning in eternity. When she makes love and dances, sparks shoot from her belly and the immortal tedium of celestial peace is relieved.

So Saint Peter didn't let him in. And Firmino did not beg, or say a word. He stood waiting in silence.

A long time has passed and Firmino is still there, waiting hat in hand, standing firm at the gates of Paradise.

From his observatory in the depths, Lucifer contemplates the situation with some consternation. Lucifer sees it coming; he groans: "I always get the worst."

Window on Beings and Doings

Smooth is the skin of the woman who irons.
    Tall and bony, the man who repairs umbrellas.
    Plucked, the woman who sells chickens.
    In the inquisitor's eyes shine demons.
    Coins lie behind the usurer's eyelids.
    The watchmaker's whiskers mark the hours.
    The janitor has keys for fingers.
    The prison guard looks like the prisoner and the psychiatrist
looks crazed.
    The hunter becomes the animal he pursues.
    Time turns lovers into twins.
    The dog walks the man who walks him.
    The tortured tortures the dreams of the torturer.
    The poet flees from the metaphor in the mirror.

Story of the Apostle Saint Peter in America

Firmino waits, leaning on his rifle, while the virtuous zoom into heaven without so much as a greeting.

"This is no life," says the dead man.

Firmino is not about to spend all eternity with no one to talk to, listening from the edge of Paradise to his woman's laughter. The old desert warrior deserves something better than this freezing hole of humiliation. Hell has a bad reputation, they say it's another name for earth, but down there the door is open and it's warm like back home.

The bandit decides. He is about to make the leap of no return into the immense frying pan where sinners sizzle, when a miracle occurs.

The miracle: the white bars open a crack and out pokes a white beard, then a bald head. Saint Peter steps out of Paradise. The apostle is looking for a good spot from which to view the world, and from inside you just can't see it.

God's gatekeeper walks a few steps on the firm air and, squatting down, he starts to blow clouds. An enormous key ring hangs from his belt.

Firmino slips behind him and with silken fingers grabs the keys, opens the gate, and sneaks into the kingdom of the just. As he goes in, he tosses the keys over his shoulder.

Saint Peter, leaning over the world, doesn't even notice.

The prince of the apostles contemplates the glowing body of the earth navigating in the vacuum. He looks and he sighs.

He's listening to a little voice calling him from afar. But well he knows that he's not allowed to return to earth. God won't let him. Neither will God allow the rest of the fishermen from the Sea of Galilee to return, not even his own son Jesus. When they were on earth, they were beaten and chased out, they were hung from crosses, they were pierced with lances and left to bleed. Two thousand years have passed, but God does not forget.

Saint Peter's gaze travels across seas and deserts and mountains, until at last it comes to rest on a tiny valley hidden among the high peaks of the Andes. His gaze penetrates the night in the town of Chimpawaylla.

In the candlelight of the Chimpawaylla church, shadows tremble.

Up on the altar, Benito the priest waits for Gloria the nun who is on her way.

Benito the priest wears a stolen cloak, and on his head glows a golden halo that isn't his.

Flushed with fury or envy, Saint Peter curses what he sees.

Gloria the nun has not been in town long; Benito the priest has been there forever. He's spent his entire life here: in the confessional, reveling in other people's sins; in the pulpit, threatening the Indians with hailstorms and drought and other forms of divine vengeance.

When Gloria the nun first came, her only baggage was her mother's ring on her finger.

On her deathbed, her mother put the ring in her husband's palm. And with her final breath she uttered a last request. Gloria's father swore never to sleep with another unless her finger fit that ring.

A few days later, out of curiosity or playfulness, Gloria put on the ring and could never get it off.

Gloria fled her house and her fate. And she became a nun.

No sooner had she donned her habit than she was assigned to the town of Chimpawaylla.

She came on foot from the mountains. She arrived at dawn, after a very long journey, with neither dust on her tunic nor fatigue in her face.

Christ's new wife knocked ever so lightly, but the caress of a knocker was enough to make Benito jump out of bed.

He opened the door and saw her: Gloria with her frightened eyes and odor of freshly fallen rain.

From that day on, Benito could not sleep without dreaming of her.

Gloria the nun swept and scraped and scrubbed, and scrubbed again, doing battle with the grime of centuries that covered the church. Now the clothes of the saints smell of sunshine.

Several times Gloria washed Saint Peter, and each time she hugged his feet and, kneeling down, entreated him to liberate her defiled hand from the ring that condemned her.

This morning Benito told her of the apostle's impending visit: "When night falls, Saint Peter will speak to you."

From that moment, Gloria has been unable to sit still. She spent the day pacing the outskirts of town, searching for a little peace for her soul. Swept up in euphoria, she failed to hear the warnings. She didn't listen to the paca-paca bird whistling bad omens from the top of a willow, or the duck screaming admonitions from the waters of the lake.

Meanwhile, Benito undressed the statue of Saint Peter and hid him in the garret. He put on the saint's cloak. Then he shaved his head and donned a beard made of fibers of white wool. He climbed up on the altar. And there he stayed, to the right of the cross, motionless, waiting.

Night falls. And when at last the Lord's prettiest lamb approaches, trembling, Saint Peter raises his arms and speaks. Softly, almost in a whisper, he says: "Grandpa God has commanded me to sleep at your side and take off your ring."

Gloria faints.

She is awakened by fingers caressing her forehead and stroking her hair.

The white hood slips and falls.

"God wants us naked in body and soul," whispers Saint Peter.

"May his will be done."

And thus the rooster crows in the midst of night.

And high above and far away, the other Saint Peter covers his eyes.

Later, he tries to stand up. His back cracks. He feels dizzy. His mouth is full of forbidden words.

Still bent over, the apostle pats his sore waist and discovers, then, that he no longer has the keys to the kingdom of heaven.

Window on Walls

Written on a wall in Montevideo: *Nothing in vain. All in wine.*

Also in Montevideo: *Virgins have many Christmases, but no christenings.*

In Buenos Aires: *I'm so ungry I ate the h.*

Also in Buenos Aires: *We will revive even if it kills us!*

In Quito: *When we had all the answers, they changed the questions.*

In Mexico: *Give the president minimum wage, so he too can feel the rage.*

In Lima: *We don't want to survive. We want to live.*

In Havana: *You can dance to anything.*

In Rio de Janeiro: *He who is afraid of living is never born.*

Window on Latin American Tabloids

Distraught with Jealousy, Man Makes
Bloody Hamburger of Tender Dove

> *Commits Suicide by Leaping*
> *From Eighth Floooooooooor*

DRINKING TOO MUCH
MADE HIM GAY!

> *Painting Stolen from Blind Artist.*
> *Painted by Ear.*

A TWIN BROTHER IS GROWING IN HIS STOMACH!

Elderly Man Dies at the Movies
Watching Sophia's Tits

KILLED HIS MOTHER
WITHOUT GOOD CAUSE!

> Man Dies Crushed
> By His Own Address

Window on Soap Opera

"The Right to be Born" was the most popular radio drama of all times. That midcentury melodrama unleashed many serious floods of Latin American tears.

"So why do you make people cry so much?" the author was asked.

And Félix B. Caignet defended himself: "I don't make anybody cry. I just give them a pretext."

Story of the Child Who Saved Himself from Mother's Love and Other Dangers

An egg was floating on the Uspanapa River.

Caridad fished her hand in the water to catch it, and leaned over so far that she fell head first into the muddy depths.

After a lot of kicking, up she came soaked and eggless, spouting water and rage from all seven orifices of her face. She climbed out onto the bank, knocked into some low branches, and the egg, which she had seen reflected in the river, fell from the tree and landed at her feet.

Caridad sat down. The heat of her body cracked the egg and a bellowing Andancio was born.

Her tongue darted out like a snake's. She licked her lips and contemplated the growing child: "Mine, mine," she said.

Andancio was grateful because, after all, she had brought him into the world. But whenever Caridad went out, the child confided his worries to a mouse: "My mama wants to eat me."

The mouse would nod: "All mothers get like that."

At the gossip corner in that town in Veracruz, Caridad complained to her neighbors: "I give up. That ingrate won't gain weight. Sacrifice, sacrifice. What's the point of my sacrifice?"

All the food went to the child. Caridad got so hungry that she starting eating the clay walls of the house. The walls got thinner with each supper, and all the clay pots disappeared down her throat, except for the big one.

Every evening Caridad brought water and fanned the fire. When the water started to steam she tossed in a handful of salt. Then she went to the corner where Andancio slept: "Show me your finger."

Andancio would proffer the mouse's tail. Caridad would squeeze it, grow blind with fury, then go off muttering.

Thanks to the mouse, who dug a hole in the thin wall, Andancio managed to escape.

He walked without looking back and by dawn was deep in the forest.

From the top of a palm tree, he saw his house in flames.

Caridad had kicked the burning logs and the fire had taken revenge.

The neighbors wrapped Caridad's ashes in a shroud and sent a toad to throw them into the swamp.

When Andancio saw the toad coming, jumping along with a sack on his back, he blocked his way. He needed that sack, for you only have one mother in life: in the struggle, the shroud fell open and Caridad's ashes took flight.

Chased by the black cloud, Andancio ran and dove into the river. Thus he was saved by the mirror which had offered his first reflection.

The toad, who was slower, could not defend himself from that army of lances, and was left with his skin forever pocked with bites.

Since then we have been tormented by mosquitoes.

Window on Invisible Dictatorships

The sacrificing mother exercises the dictatorship of servitude.

The solicitous friend exercises the dictatorship of favors.

Charity exercises the dictatorship of debt.

Free markets allow us to accept the prices imposed on us.

Free expression allows us to listen to those who speak in our name.

Free elections allow us to choose the sauce with which we will be eaten.

Story of the Mosquito Miracle

The town priest used to tell him: "You're the only black man with a white soul."

Montón sold his soul to God. In return for immortality, he was condemned to a life of goodness.

He had been living his saintly and eternal life for quite a while when the carnival began, as it does every year, in the town of Saint Marc. As with every year, Montón shut himself behind locks and bars, and resigned himself to fasting and mortification.

Outside, meanwhile, the fiesta flourished. Feverish drumming tossed a steamy whirlwind of bodies into the air, the music danced them, returned them to earth, and sent them flying once more.

This lasted until Tuesday at midnight. Then the time of pleasure ended and the hour of repentance and duty arrived.

The moon was full. The tide rose, birds hid from view, the air grew chilly, and Montón came out of seclusion.

Seated in a rocking chair, in the fresh night air, Montón was drinking a glass of pure rainwater when suddenly the moon got into his glass and it shattered.

The entire town of Saint Marc was drowned in liquor. Rivers of rum sprang from the shattered glass and everyone got drunk and dizzy that night and in the days that followed. Since then, Saint Marc's carnival begins when it ends everywhere else, on Ash Wednesday.

It was during those days that Montón lost his hat. And then he lost his woman: one morning he touched that statue of ice and realized she was a bit colder than usual.

While shovelfuls of earth fell on the casket, Montón mumbled the rosary of the fifteen mysteries, and could not keep his lips from beseeching God: "Don't even think of sending her back."

The gravedigger shoveled dirt and more dirt until his arms ached, but the hole remained. All the dirt in the world would not have filled its depths. They had no choice but to plant the cross down below, in the middle of that open mouth.

"The earth is still hungry," declared the gravedigger, who was said to be wise.

Montón giggled nervously. His head spun, his knees failed him, and he fainted.

Relatives and neighbors fanned the widower, victim of the noonday heat or the sorrow of irredeemable loss.

A few days later, Montón noticed that his body gave off someone else's shadow. By daylight or firelight, the shadow of some other body grew from his and went where it shouldn't. And from Montón's body blew a crazy wind that knocked the prayerbook from his hands, made flutes play and women's skirts balloon.

Montón, who had always been a man of spare diet, started devouring things with implacable hunger: his own and others', raw and cooked, still and moving. The enemy of tobacco puffed nonstop; the devotee of water drank hard liquor. Eating and drinking and smoking, he became delirious and spouted nonsense to his dumbfounded grandchildren.

The boys suspected the evil eye. And they decided to move the house. They pulled it up by its stakes and took it, walls, roof, and all, to the other end of town. They spread eggshells on the ground, raised a cow's skull in the middle of the lot, and hung a wreath of garlic around the neck of their grieving grandfather.

Things got worse. Now the martyr of the working life spent night and day lying in the sweet hammock of any woman's breast, stoking

himself up with lovemaking until light shone right through him. On the altar of his house, where Christ on the cross used to hang, Montón planted a tree of Paradise, red with fruit and filled with birds, in homage to lovers unplagued by navels, or memory, or duty.

People get sick from above, like plants. Montón's grandchildren decided their grandfather was sick in the head. Since his condition was only getting worse, they took him to the Big Goat.

The Big Goat used his beard for a sheet. If you yanked on his beard while he slept, he would talk.

Montón's grandchildren posed their question. And with the first pull, the Big Goat revealed the truth: "Mosquitoes," he murmured without waking.

The boys did not understand. They did not remember that one morning, some time back, their grandfather had awakened swollen with bites.

Those mosquitoes were responsible. They sucked so much of his blood that they performed a transfusion. Montón got the blood of a famous sinner named Fefé. It was a case of an incurable soul switch. Montón was left as he now was, and Fefé, once a tireless enjoyer, became incapable of adventure, condemned to repeat the same day, day after day, unable to drink without throwing up, or make love without guilt, or feel without thinking.

Window on the Word (IV)

Magda Lemonnier clips words out of the newspapers, words of all sizes, and she keeps them in boxes. In red boxes, angry words. Loving words in a green box. Neutral ones in a blue box. Sad ones in a yellow box. And in a transparent box she keeps words that are magical.

Sometimes she opens the boxes and upends them on the table, so the words can mix as they please. Then the words tell her what is happening and foretell what will occur.

Story of the Archangel's Return

Montón's life became a carnival, an eternal dance in the air. One day, as he celebrated the mosquitoes' mischief, he heard someone behind him clear his throat. He turned around, but saw no one.

"Give yourself up."

He looked down and burst out laughing. There stood an ugly shriveled-up dwarf dressed as a policeman.

The archangel cut his laughter off cold. "God sent me," he said. "You've heard of Him? I have orders to take you prisoner."

Faced with the weight of the evidence, the unfortunate man paled. Until that moment death had been like sickness or old age, something that happened only to others.

"The going-away party," he stuttered, and his trembling hand poured out two shots of white rum.

"I shouldn't," muttered the dwarf, emptying his glass in one gulp.

One drink followed another: "We are moments, that's all, little nothings," Montón sighed. After a pause the archangel concurred, nodding his head: "Fear rules."

In the candlelight Montón's body, grew large, a body the color of its shadow, a shadow which grew along with its body.

When he opened the second bottle, the old black man got up the courage to ask: "Have you been at this long?"

The emissary of the Lord clucked his tongue and said nothing.

But as the rum went down, the words poured out. The archangel recalled the old days in Comayagua, the good life worth living, glorious and fleeting, and he told how the winged agents of the Great Beyond had kidnapped him: "They took me back."

Now he was barred from redemptive missions, and could only visit the earth to retrieve those condemned to die.

In the middle of telling his troubles, he fell asleep.

When he awoke, dawn was breaking. The archangel suddenly remembered his job: "Dust, ashes, nothing," warned the voice of duty, hoarse from the hangover.

Montón, who had not fled, rocked peacefully in a rocking chair. "If you want to take me with you, you'll have to untie me," he said.

And with two fingers he held up a woman's hair from neither the head nor the armpit. "Cut it," he insisted. "I can't."

The archangel tried. He tried with his teeth, and with the blade of a knife, and with the blows of an ax. That hair would not be cut.

The archangel requested instructions from the heavens.

Saint Michael tore out his feathers in anger. His screams shook the galaxies: the chief of the archangels cursed the idiot who fell for a trick as old as the world, a trick everyone knows, and he swore that he would send that good-for-nothing to hell.

But the heavenly hierarchy ordered the affair closed. Satan doesn't accept guests without God's signature. And no one dared bother Our Lord with a tale so humiliating and worthy of forgetting. New wars and revolutions were breaking out every day in the infinite and turbulent universe, and God was not in the mood for anything unpleasant.

The recidivist functionary, who had repeatedly shown himself to be careless, inept, and corrupt, was chained to a cloud and sentenced to listen for all eternity to the angels' chorus rehearsing their songs of praise to the glory of the Creator and his insatiable thirst for tears.

When the archangel flew off, the horizon disappeared. The sky turned to sea and let loose a downpour.

Montón walked through the rain, through the world that the rain was awakening.

Window on Prohibitions

On a wall in a Madrid eatery hangs a sign that says: *No Singing*.

On a wall in the airport of Rio de Janeiro hangs a sign that says: *No Playing with Luggage Carts*.

Ergo: There are still people who sing, there are still people who play.

Story of the Corn House

Andancio was a homeless orphan. On a pilgrimage in search of a home on earth, he reached the shores of the Gulf of Mexico.

A bolt of lightning reared up to protect his dominions. Perched on his long incandescent tail, lightning fulminated at the intruder: "Not here!" he bellowed from the heights of his criminal prestige. And the sky thundered with rage.

Andancio pointed to the horizon. Speaking softly, as if begging pardon, he picked up a stone and challenged: whoever can throw a stone across the entire sea will be the winner.

The bolt of lightning didn't answer, but he chose a stone, reared back, and threw. The lightning's stone traced an astonishing curve across the sky, and after brushing against the sun it fell into the water, just short of the horizon.

Andancio secretly called out the dove and the woodpecker. Then his body became a bow and shot off the dove as if it were a stone, and the dove buzzed through the air and was lost from sight. A little

while later the woodpecker struck a dead tree with its beak, and that hollow blow faked the sound of the stone landing on the other shore.

The bolt of lightning hung his head. And he had to go off to where his stone had fallen. Andancio ordered the lightning to announce the beginning of the time of water on earth; and to send rain to bathe his body and make it grow.

Thus Andancio found land and rain, and he grew a tall body and leaves and ears and kernels and silk. And he was corn.

Window on Cycles

People made of corn make corn. People made of the flesh and colors of corn dig a cradle for the corn and cover it with good earth and weed it and water it and tell it words of love. And when the corn is tall, the people of corn grind it on a stone and hold it up and applaud it and lay it on a loving fire and eat it, so that inside the people of corn the corn will continue walking on the earth.

Story of the Parrot's Resurrection

The parrot fell into a steaming pot. He stuck up his head, felt dizzy, and fell back in. He fell in because he was curious, and he drowned in the hot soup.

The girl, who was his friend, cried.

The orange peeled off its skin and offered itself to console her.

The fire under the pot repented and went out.

The wall released a stone.

The tree leaning against the wall trembled with grief and all its leaves fell to the ground.

As on every other day, the wind arrived to comb the leafy tree, and found it bare. When the wind heard the story, it expelled a gusty sigh.

The gust opened the window, blew about the world aimlessly, and went to heaven.

When heaven heard the bad news, it grew pale.

And seeing the heavens go pale, the man was left speechless.

The potter of Ceará wanted to know what had happened. Finally, the man got back his tongue and told him that the parrot drowned
 and the girl cried
 and the orange peeled off its skin
 and the fire went out
 and the wall lost a stone
 and the tree lost its leaves
 and the wind lost a gust
 and the window blew open
 and heaven was left without color
 and man without words.

Then the potter brought together all that sadness. And with this material his hands managed to bring the dead back to life.

The parrot born from grief had red feathers from the fire
and blue feathers from the sky
and green feathers from the leaves of the tree
and a beak hard from the stone and golden from the orange
and he had human words to speak
and water from the tears to drink and feel refreshed
and he had an open window for escaping
and off he flew in the gust of wind.

Window on Memory (I)

On the shores of another sea, an old potter retires.

His eyes cloud over, his hands tremble, the hour to say goodbye has arrived. Then the ceremony of initiation begins: the old potter offers the young potter his best piece. As tradition dictates among the Indians of northwest America, the outgoing artist gives his master work to the incoming one.

And the young potter doesn't keep that perfect vase to contemplate or admire: he smashes it on the ground, breaks it into a thousand pieces, picks up the pieces, and incorporates them into his own clay.

Story of the Shadow

The first taste he remembers was a carrot.

The first smell, a lime cut in half.

He remembers that he cried when he discovered distance.

And he remembers the morning he discovered his shadow.

That morning he saw what, until then, he had looked at without seeing: stuck to his feet lay a shadow longer than his body.

He walked, he ran. Wherever he went, no matter where, the shadow pursued him.

He wanted to get rid of it. He wanted to step on it, kick it, beat it; but the shadow, quicker than his legs and arms, always managed to elude him. He wanted to jump over it, but it always jumped ahead. Turning swiftly, he got rid of it in front, but it reappeared in back. He hugged close to a tree trunk, leaned up against a wall, ducked behind a door. Wherever he hid, the shadow found him.

At last he managed to break free. He took a flying leap, stretched out in a hammock, and separated himself from his shadow.

It lay under the net, waiting for him.

Later he found out that clouds, night, and noon suppress shadows. And he found out that shadows always come back, coaxed by the sun, like a ring in search of your finger, or a coat traveling toward your body.

And he got used to it.

When he grew, his shadow grew with him. And he was afraid of losing it.

Time passed. And now that he is shrinking, in the final days of his life, he is afraid of dying and leaving it alone.

Window on the Invisible Face

Everything has, we all have, a face and a mark. Dogs and snakes and sea gulls, you and I, those who are living and those who have already lived, and all who walk, wriggle, or fly: we all have a face and a mark.

That's what the Mayas believe. And they believe that the mark, the invisible mark, is more of a face than the visible face. By your mark you'll be known.

Window on the Kingdom That Was

In Sayomal, the grandmother said, way way way back in ancient times, trees and people didn't dry up. When the first pain hurt, no one knew if it was red or black or white. When the first death occurred, no one had a name for it. When the lands of Sayomal were invaded by the shadows of pain and death, the sun chose a man and saved him, yanked him aside with its rays. And ever since, he has been alone, outside time, sleeping in the sun's sanctuary which drifts above the horizon.

"The last one from Sayomal," the grandmother said, "is waiting for you."

Story of the Time That Was

Back in the time that's lost in time, the grandmother says, the deer was faster than the arrows that sought him.

The serpent wandered the earth, rattling fiestas from head to tail, and his rattles resounded each day and echoed into the past and future.

The turkey was lord of the highlands, and his cry carried into the farthest corners.

When the time of misfortune arrived in Yucatán, the deer no longer ran like the wind, he got hurt and cried. His liquid eyes, which provided the rest of the wounded with something to drink, were left moist and large forever.

The serpent lost his rattles of joy. Since then, his nude body only rattles out fear.

And the turkey fell to the lowlands where no one hears him, and never again was he able to fly from this earth where the outcasts of heaven suffer in exile.

Window on Memory (II)

A refuge?

A belly?

A shelter to hide you when you're drowning in the rain, or shivering in the cold, or spinning in the wind?

Do we have a splendid past ahead of us?

For navigators who love the wind, memory is a port of departure.

Window on Arrival

Pilar and Daniel Weinberg's son was baptized on the coast. The baptism taught him what was sacred.

They gave him a sea shell: "So you'll learn to love the water."

They opened a cage and let a bird go free: "So you'll learn to love the air."

They gave him a geranium: "So you'll learn to love the earth."

And they gave him a little bottle sealed up tight: "Don't ever, ever open it. So you'll learn to love mystery."

Window on Departure

The great-grandchildren dress her for school. Every day at noon, that old woman drags herself out of bed, very nervous because the teacher will be angry, and demands the white apron and the blue fillet: "Hurry up, hurry up, it's getting late."

An old man copies his own childhood drawings. He made them seventy years ago. While he copies them, while he copies himself, his hand does not shake.

He keeps a few newspapers, old like himself, rolled up and tied carefully with rags. He's afraid that the words will escape.

Sofía Opalski is very old, nobody knows how old, who knows if she knows. She's got one leg and gets about in a wheelchair. Both of them are worn out, she and the chair. The chair's screws are loose, and so are hers.

When she falls, or the chair tips, Sofía pulls herself as best she can over to the telephone and dials the only number she remembers. And she asks, from the end of time: "Who am I?"

Far from Sofía, in another country, is Lucía Herrera, who was born three or four years ago. Lucía asks, from the beginning of time: "What do I want?"

Story of the Coachman

He spent the day waiting, motionless in the driver's seat, the reins in his hands. Every once in a great while a tourist would appear, someone who wanted to stick his nose in the old barrios and bygone times. And on rare occasions some family from a big house would still turn up, the ones who went to mass even if it wasn't Sunday.

Waiting, he'd doze off. And perhaps Don Antenor dreamed that his lost teeth returned to his mouth, the lost hairs returned to his head, and the fat of age dripped off his body. Or he dreamed that he was behind the wheel of a brand new Mercedes-Benz, ramrod straight in a new uniform, under a shining sign that blinked "Taxi."

When night closed in, Don Antenor would shake the reins: "Come on, Useless."

Useless didn't quicken his pace, he just moseyed on home.

Protected by darkness, Don Antenor picked up a few bags of garbage along the way.

The professor chose to sit next to the driver. He'd come from the capital to give a talk on Maimonides' cure for asthma, and he wanted to see Cartagena de Indias the best way.

They traveled in the shade of the walls and by the edge of the sea, along the lanes of the old city, under stone arches and the wooden cantilevers of overhanging balconies, then along the traffic-choked avenues of the new part of town.

At the pace set by the horse and the passing of the hours, the professor paid homage to the quiet heroism of Don Antenor, spark of the nation's memory, bastion of lost tradition: "You are part of the historical patrimony of our country," he praised him, and with a few slaps of his palm he congratulated his back.

When the trip was over, the professor stayed on a while to talk. He looked deep into Don Antenor's eyes and prescribed Hogg's cod-liver oil. And when he climbed off the coach he asked how much he owed.

The answer offended him: "So little you value your work as a coachman and the sacrifice of the noble beast that accompanies you?"

And he went off without paying, very angry, and disappeared around the first corner.

Don Antenor chased the hounds out of his soul by insulting Useless and making the whip whistle over his ears.

Every day there was less day. Every day it grew dark earlier. His daily bread moved farther out of reach every day: the fish swam very deep, the birds flew very high.

But Don Antenor was still there. For better or for worse, there he was in the plaza. Just as in the olden days, when the streets were full of comings and goings, noise and bustle, but without machines or almost without them. Back then, the Kaiser coach was a carriage for the First Lady, and for matadors and tenors from Spain, masters of bullfights and zarzuelas; it took women with fans to gala balls. The Kaiser sported gold letters on its doors, Ventanía whinnied with glee, and Don Antenor knew the secrets of bedrooms and lawyers' chambers, the lives and miracles of the finer people.

Those people didn't exist anymore, and neither did the things they wanted; but Don Antenor was there. And so was the Kaiser, full of holes and limping on one wheel. And so was that wretched nag, so unlike Ventanía, who used to strike sparks on the cobblestones and stamp out the beat of a triumphal march. Useless just wandered, half asleep, around and around the plaza, while automobiles roared in the vertigo of traffic.

When the day of the Virgin of Candelaria arrived, a multitude climbed in procession up to the summit of the high hill where she lives. Don Antenor went as well. He crawled on bloody knees, blinded by sun and dust, and begged for a miracle. He asked her to close the wounds in his soul, the ones that wouldn't heal: he spoke in the childhood whisper he used when he called her my girlfriend, my come-sit-by-me, and she gave him the walls that surround the old city.

But the Virgin was busy opening roads in the sea, resuscitating the drowned, and taking fish to empty nets. That year there were many evil deeds on the water, a lot of work for the Lady of Navigators, and she didn't have time for bad luck on dry land.

While Don Antenor was praying up above, crying into her deaf ear, Useless was down below, tied up to the Kaiser, frying in the sun. It was a ferocious sun even in the shade had there been any. Useless chewed a little dry grass, bit the bridle, and cursed that old brute who treated him as if he were made of wood; he had spent his life in the cinch with his mouth shut and the very least he deserved was a hat with colored feathers and a banquet of purple corn, alfalfa stalks, fresh clover, oatmeal puree.

That night, Useless escaped. Sick of chewing dirt and sadness with thorns for dessert, he escaped. He wanted to gallop, to take off cross-country and lose himself in the verdure and roll on the ground and eat his fill of fresh grass and neigh until he fell dumb.

He wanted to gallop and he did in that headlong flight, the longest gallop of his life.

Beyond the suburbs, he tripped and fell. With difficulty he managed to get up: his hooves hesitated, his chest boomed, his wounded body groaned. Useless had to resign himself to his tired old way of walking. And step by step he continued his flight, until he collapsed under overhanging branches by the coast.

The carpenter was adjusting the spokes of a wheel around the axle when he looked up and saw him. Don Antenor was approaching. In the cloud of summer dust, he cut a twisted figure: frayed penguin frock coat, memory of a top hat, bow tie with faded wings. He came around the bend in the road, hitched to the poles, dragging his coach. The Kaiser lurched along, screeching like broken wire springs, and Don Antenor sweated profusely.

Soon the carpenter would finish the wheel. Collapsed in the shade of the carriage, Don Antenor told him that he'd resolved to do without the services of his horse. His business was taking a new turn. Now he'd move things, make deliveries, whatever.

Days went by, weeks. Useless went marauding in his old haunts. Every day he watched Don Antenor and the Kaiser go out, one pulling the other, and by the trail of their scent he could tell where they were going.

Useless hesitated. He walked about, tried to move off, but kept coming back. He licked his skinned bony leg, and he hesitated. He scratched his ribs with his hoof and went on hesitating. He chewed the grass, chewed over his doubts, lay down near the bare shed that had been his home and slept.

And one day, one dawn, Useless pushed open the door with his muzzle. The faint light was sufficient to reveal his straw bed and the harness that hung from the rafters.

Don Antenor climbed out of the Kaiser. The spindly legs below his ghostly nightshirt barely held him up. He pointed to the trough filled with water. "Over there you've got some," he grunted.

"I drink beer," said the horse.

Window on Goodbye

He couldn't sleep. He'd saved all his dreams in a shopping bag, and the bag had fallen open and the dreams escaped, and he could no longer sleep because he had no more dreams to dream.

That's what he said. He also said that he'd lost two days, a Monday and a Tuesday, and he looked for them desperately but those days were nowhere to be found.

His agony was not short-lived. He had less and less air. Toward the end, crucified by tubes, all he could do was babble, "What a long hill to climb."

And he died without having found his dreams or the days he'd had and lost.

He didn't have much else. Fernando Rodríguez never wanted to have. He owned nothing, a naked man; and he went about naked, chased by children and crazy people and birds.

Story of the Shoemaker
Who Fled from His Creditors

"Name and surname?"

No answer.

The police chief rapped on his chest three times: "Are you dead?"

Cándido lay silent. The authority declared him a cadaver.

With his eyes rolled back to watch his eyebrows, Cándido lay wondering. Just one little thought cloud floated over his head: "Suppose they bury the casket with me in it?"

A local poet given to socialist realism immortalized the unhappy shoemaker at once in a seven-verse acrostic. The poet sang of the unfortunate life of the deceased who broke his back hammering leather day and night to feed his ungrateful family and who the more he worked the less he earned and the more he owed.

His neighbors and relatives, on the other hand, recalled his aversion to the sweat of his brow, an allergy that produced nausea and a rash. According to them, the cobbler had never so much as put on half a sole. He preferred to earn a living by selling every so often a

jar filled with air from Paris, or a bottle of Brazilian soil kissed by
the Pope, or wooden spoons good for stealing food from the blind.

   That's what they said; I don't know. But it's a fact that when
Cándido took that tragic step, he owed a candle to every saint. With
his own hands he knocked together a pine coffin, polished it, put on
a hasp that bore his name, and gave himself up for dead from a death
well died.

The wake was held in the church. Lots of debts, no debtor. Cándido was mourned by his numerous creditors and by no one else. Stiff in the casket, arms crossed over his chest, he listened to his victims moan until everybody he had strung along left the temple. Then he heard nothing but the murmur of some devout woman who prayed forgiveness for the sins she never committed. And when night fell, the dead man was left alone.

He waited, and at last he decided. He rubbed his sore eyes and very slowly he put one foot outside the casket. Then the other. When he sat up, the casket creaked. Index finger to his lips, he told himself: "Shh."

He started walking, step by step. Barefoot, he made his way about the darkened church. Under the cross, under Jesus, between Mary Magdalene and the Virgin Mary, he found a good place to sit down. He pulled a cigarette out of the pocket of his shroud and lit up with a wax taper. And that's what he was doing, smoking and celebrating, when he heard noises and had to scramble back into the coffin.

While the robbers emptied the altar, stripped the walls, and undressed the saints, the shoemaker mouthed silent Our Fathers and Ave Marias and macumba spells. But the leader of the bandits grew curious: "Maybe this body has a gold tooth?"

When Cándido felt that claw patting his jaw, he bit down with all his heart and soul then sat straight up in the casket.

The thief, cross-eyed, fell spread-eagled to the floor and the whole gang fled in a howl, leaving angels' wings and silks and silver scattered behind them.

The entire town came out to venerate the new Lazarus.

Everyone brought him offerings. People came with hens under their arms and bags of beans and the shiniest of ornaments. Even his creditors kissed his feet.

From his throne in Paradise, the Divine Father had deigned to cast a glance at this little village lost in the solitudes of Alagoas. And he had chosen the most humble of his sons to save the temple, his house, his body, violated by the children of Satan.

He who had come back to life became a holy miracle worker.

Cándido charged for his miracles in advance. He was no cheap saint. "What do they want?" he'd grumble. "A favor from God for the price of a banana?"

According to the surviving witnesses, all his earnings ended up with the pimps and gaming houses in the far-off city of Maceió. Contemplating the obolus in the palm of his hand, Cándido would declare: "Why are coins round? So they can roll."

Thus the years went by.
     The hungry received no inheritance,
     the cripples did not walk,
     the bald did not sprout hair,
     the old maids did not marry,
     it did not rain in the desert,
     the dwarfs did not grow.
     And one day, Cándido died. And he did not wake up.

Eduardo Galeano

Window on the Sea

It's not fixed in one spot. The fate of mountains and trees lies in the roots, but the sea, like us, is condemned to a wandering life.

Sailors at heart: we, men of the coast, are made of sea as well as earth. And we know it well, even if we're unaware of it when we navigate the waves of city streets from café to café, and travel through the mist toward the port or shipwreck that awaits us tonight.

Story of the Rowdy Warlocks of the Southern Sea

In the old days, witchcraft was a frequent visitor to the islands of Chiloé.

When the warlocks didn't feel like flying, they came mounted on an immense sea horse that spewed waves of foam and foul tempers from its nostrils. They'd dismount at midnight, hopping on one leg, and with pocket mirrors point out the ones chosen for their evil deeds. From far off they looked like leaping flames: under their ponchos they wore burning vests made of the skin of the dead soaked in human fat, and with these lanterns they lit up the path.

It wasn't always like that. Sometimes they'd turn into toothy fish that swam on dry land and had a hankering for Christian flesh. Other times they'd appear in the form of bats that would fly about in search of necks worthy of their thirst. Those ghostly owls who opened incurable wounds in everything they looked at were transfigured warlocks, and warlocks too were the crows who cackled insults and impregnated virgins with the touch of their wings.

On the islands, they stole women. Their witch hands, fires of hell, were the best medicine for the frosts of winter, and more than a few mass-a-day ladies dreamed of being kidnapped.

When they tired of orgies to redeem pious women, the warlocks would leave their coral palaces in the depths of the sea. They'd emerge from the waters, their skin shining with sargassum, and head off in a ghost ship.

Between the Isle of Seagulls and Tierra del Fuego, many fishermen saw that splendor of red sails burst forth from the sea and vanish into the black mist; and they heard echoes of the rollicking music and a thousand laughs from the endless festivities on board. And more than one local swore with his fingers on the cross that the ghost ship came into port at Tren-Tren, chased by a swarm of monstrous birds, to repair the hull damaged on remote forays, or that the ship plied the seas near the caves of Quincaví, where the warlocks picked up water from the cascading spring that erases baptisms.

In those days, the ghost ship was a joy of the night.

At a certain dateless point and in a certain mapless place, they found what others sought. They found it by accident. As the Annals of Warlock History affirm, they were frolicking in the far reaches when they happened upon an island wrapped in shimmering vapors, glowing with gold in the middle of the night.

The warlocks disembarked followed by their loyal toads, and their one-legged hops raised gold dust in the golden air. On the island there was no one. As they marched toward a mountain of gold, along the golden edge of a ravine, the warlocks saw gold growing in the fields and gardens, golden furze, oranges of gold, grapevines weighty with bunches of gold, and they saw old skeletons still clinging to axes and swords. The path was strewn with dry bones and helmets and armor and muskets covered with rust. Who knows how many years ago the hidalgos and their conquistador troops had fallen, stabbing each other on the path that led to the crests of El Dorado.

The warlocks never came back.

Sometimes the wind brings the murmurs of distant litanies and they're not from suffering souls, or the drowned, or the shipwrecked who drift about tortured by hunger and cold. On the unbewitched coasts of Chiloé, those who understand the wind know the laments come from the ghost ship. They claim the warlocks were condemned to watch over the gold and to watch over each other. The ship circles the island without ever stopping and without ever leaving its ring of foam. Its sails have lost their sea legs. And not even the wind will come near that gloomy prison that creaks in the fog.

Ships that dare approach are left suddenly dry, navigating in a vacuum, and the indiscreet sailors float back to land turned into timbers from a shipwreck.

Window on a Successful Man

He can't look at the moon without calculating the distance.
   He can't look at a tree without calculating the firewood.
   He can't look at a painting without calculating the price.
   He can't look at a menu without calculating the calories.
   He can't look at a man without calculating the advantage.
   He can't look at a woman without calculating the risk.

Story of the Intruder

And on the seventh day, God rested.
And He recovered all of his strength.
And on the eighth day, He made her.

Genesis 2.1

You came down the river on the night of your wedding. The whole town was on the dock, mouths agape, when you emerged from the darkness standing erect on foam. The splashing water pressed your white tunic to your body and a tiara of live fireflies lit up your face.

Lucho Cabalgante had traded six cows for you, all he owned, so that your beauty would heal his body aggrieved by solitude and humiliated by age.

That night was a party. And at dawn, under a rain of rice, the raft turned four times on the river and off you went, the two of you, chased by the farewells of guitars and maracas.

The following night, the raft returned. You were standing. Lucho Cabalgante was stretched out as flat as could be.

Lucho died without touching you, while your white tunic slid slowly down the length of your body and fell in a heap at your feet. As he watched you, his breast burst.

They kept vigil with the body covered because he was all purple and his tongue was hanging out. And during the wake, Lucho's two brothers stabbed each other fighting for the inheritance, a lone female, unconquered and widowed.

They had to dig three graves.

You stayed on in town.

The father of the dead never missed a step. From the shore, old Cabalgante followed you with his spyglass while you made the eddies sing; at dawn, you turned your broad oar in the water and a hoarse music emanated from the foam. Your water-bubble song was more powerful than the church bell. The canoe danced, the fish came out, and all men awoke.

In the market, you traded shad and haddock for mango and pine-apple and palm oil. The old man followed you, limping along with his rheumatism, spying on your steps. And when you lay back in your hammock, he spied on your dreams.

The old man couldn't eat or sleep. Bleeding from jealousy, a cloud of mosquitoes biting him day and night, he lost his flesh and his breath. And when all that was left of him was a handful of silent bones, they buried him beside his sons.

You didn't wear dresses from Chez Paris, or bracelets, or earrings, or rings, or even a clip for your long black hair, always shiny from banana-root baths.

But every time you came near Escolástico, who was paralyzed, he jumped. There you were going down the streets of the town, impervious to all the dust and clay, and Escolástico felt that fate was calling him, shouting to him, ordering him to enter your body and remain there for all the days of all the years of his life.

"What am I doing here, outside of her?" Escolástico tormented himself until one morning, when he saw you go by, he leapt out of his wheelchair, ran, and died, struck by a bicycle.

When the tide was high, the river reached up to his chest: Fortunato could sink any boat with one arm, and with two he'd raise it up again. Insatiable devourer of raw fish and fresh women, he was a Samson who boasted: "My sword of hairy hilt only makes boy children."

A bolt of lightning destroyed him when he was about to make his move on you. The lightning, which came out of a cloudless sky, caught Fortunato with his sword stiff and his arms outstretched at the edge of the hammock where you slept; but you went on sleeping peacefully, aware of nothing, and of Fortunato all that was left was a carbon pillar with three points sticking out.

Drawn by your reputation, news of which had spread all along the Pacific coast, a journalist and a photographer from the port of Buenaventura came to town.

It was a night of dancing. You were twisting in the air at the center of a round of applause, shoulders still, hips gyrating, those feet of yours whirring and whirring, hummingbird wings, and the foam of your petticoats rising up in waves over your dark and radiant thighs. The journalist managed to mutter:

"What luck,
to have been in the world,
to have seen her,"
and those were his last words.

The photographer went crazy. Trying to capture your image, winged woman, earth and sky, root and flight, he was left stuttering and trembling forever. He photographed statues and they came out blurry.

Father Jovino caught a whiff of the sea and found you nearby. He threw a handful of dirt in front, uttered his prayer making the sign of the cross, and threw another handful of dirt behind. When he saw that you were coming toward the church, he closed the door with two locks and barred it with one iron bar and one wooden one.

"Father," you said.

He backed off, aghast. On the altar, he hugged the cross.

"Father," you repeated, up against the door.

"Dear God, don't abandon me!" the priest implored, sweating buckets, burning from the fires of his perdition.

You had come to confess. You left. You were crying mint tears.

The next day, Father Jovino covered himself with blessed clay and threw himself in the river, in the deep bend, tied to Christ.

Soon they pulled both of them out. The priest was drowned and little Jesus, who before had sweated, bled, and winked, stopped blinking and no longer exuded water or blood, or performed any miracles.

Women always looked at you with furrowed brows. Ever since you came to town, the rain didn't rain and men worked little and died a lot. Someone saw spurs on your sandals and someone saw you in a cloud of sulfur. It was public and evident that the river boiled and steamed where you passed, and fish followed you frenetically waving their fins; and people knew that a snake visited you every night, slithering toward your hammock from the palm-frond roof, and it did your bidding.

The entire town condemned you, disdainful witch who'd rather laugh than pray, for your arts of enchantment and witchcraft, or for the crime of your unpardonable beauty.

And one night you left. In your canoe, standing on the foam, you vanished in the mist. No one saw you. Only I saw you. I was just a child and you didn't even notice. I see you still.

Window on the Goddess of the Sea

Iemanyá lives in the depths of the waters. There she receives offerings. On the day of her fiesta, the fishermen of Bahía sing the praises of the flirtatious and gluttonous goddess, and from their boats they lavish flattering gifts.

When she likes the presents, she offers them the favors of her protection. When she rejects the white flowers and mirrors and fans and combs and perfumes and sweets and throws them back on sandy beaches, the fishermen tremble: they'll have a bad year, a year of few fish and much danger, and more than one will get swallowed up on the high seas so that Iemanyá can calm her female furies and hungers.

Window on the Body

The Church says: *The body is a sin.*
  Science says: *The body is a machine.*
  Advertising says: *The body is a business.*
  The body says: *I am a fiesta.*

Story of the Man Who Wanted to Be Pregnant

Women? An inferior race like the blacks, the poor, and the mad. Like children, unsuited for freedom. Destined to cry and scream, to speak ill of their neighbors, and to change their minds and their hairdos daily. In bed and in the kitchen, they sometimes give pleasure. Anywhere else they inspire nothing but disgust.

Don Seráfico had always been a man of straightforward ideas. But now, in the twilight of his life, a dark cloud troubled his thoughts. Something about the Eves generated neither contempt nor pity. Hard as it was to admit, he envied them: they could be inhabited, and he could not; they could be two, and he could not. Don Seráfico never complained about life, it had given him plenty of fun and

fortune; but he had never had a baby, and he hated other people's privileges. He was not going to leave the world without having experienced the act of giving birth: "I'm going to have a son," he swore, "or if nothing else, a daughter."

On that very day another vow was made in a nearby forest. A tiger fell into a trap set by hunters. The tiger begged for help from a little monkey who was hanging from a branch, swinging back and forth. Kissing the air, the tiger promised: "I'll be your slave."

The monkey released him and the two set off. The tiger went first, clearing a path and sweeping the ground on which the monkey walked. When the monkey sat down to rest, the tiger fanned him with a banana leaf.

Don Seráfico went into Doña Juana Obánla's store, laid a stack of bills at her feet, and specified that he did not want a wife, but neither did he want a husband, a seafaring lover, or the Holy Spirit.

Juana Obánla was the magician of Camajuaní. With neither seashells nor cards nor crystal balls, she could foretell good times, alleviate bad times, and make the impossible possible.

The magician scratched her head and pondered. She remained absorbed, ruminating on possibilities, until she remembered that children are made of the same material as dreams and nightmares. Then she prepared the potion: seven heaping spoonfuls of carbon, seventeen of hydrogen, one of nitrogen, and three of oxygen.

For the entire day, the tiger was a loyal flunky. But when night fell, the feline laid his paw on the shoulder of the simian. Not to embrace him, but to hold him down. Tapping himself on the chest, he observed that we tigers do not devour the moon only because we take pity on the night. The monkey replied that it wouldn't do you much good to eat my diseased meat, infected with malaria, syphilis, and AIDS.

"We all have to die of something," the tiger reflected, while the monkey slipped free and in one leap disappeared.

Nine moons passed.

Don Seráfico had no son or daughter in his belly, but he was filled with the commotion of two hundred and seventy nights of relentless turmoil. As soon as he put his head on the pillow and closed his eyes, his dreams flung him into endless exertion:

He ran the entire night with a crazy train on his heels,

or he scrambled up a soapy pole while down below crocodiles opened their jaws wide,

or he spent the whole night making love to the eleven thousand virgins of the guardians of Our Lady of Caridad del Cobre: one after the other they clambered onto his back and did the belly dance, then rolled him over and threw themselves naked into his arms.

He would wake in a pitiful state, drag himself into the bathroom and throw cold water on his face, terrified that instead of water, words or lizards would spring from the tap.

When the ninth moon lit up the thicket, both tiger and monkey were filthy and exhausted; but the striped hunter would not give up the search for his fugitive supper. Under his tired footsteps the dry leaves crackled. His ears still buzzed, anticipating the fatal leap. His hoarse roars offered the runaway saliva to get you good and wet, tongue to corner you, teeth to grind you to bits. So passed the days, a time of many hues; and so passed the nights, a time of many scents.

Now Don Seráfico had two problems: he still hadn't given birth and he suffered the curse of incessant dreaming.

He traveled to the city, pinning his hopes on science. He paid double the fee to the highest eminence.

Doctor Bonfín listened to his story without raising an eyebrow. Don Seráfico explained that he had decided to bear from his own bowels, without a woman, the prince who would crown his lineage. And he promised to give everything he owned in return for the secret of masculine pregnancy. Doctor Bonfín warned him: "Giving birth hurts."

He put a funnel in his mouth and a cork in his anus. He had the patient lie down and he emptied into the funnel an entire bottle of castor oil.

Then Don Seráfico wanted to know what to take to shake off the nightmares that tormented him. Doctor Bonfín only asked if he slept with his arms on top of the blankets or covered up, and if he slept with hands open or clenched.

Don Seráfico never closed his eyes again for the rest of his life; but he left the doctor's office that afternoon in an advanced state of pregnancy.

At a prudent distance from the enemy, the monkey lay down for a nap at the top of a guacimo tree.

He was dozing when he heard the groans of a human and looked down: a bulbous man was squatting below, his enormous belly resting on the ground. Don Seráfico moaned and sweated fire and ice.

The monkey slid down to earth and silently contemplated the spectacle.

When the cork popped and that balloon burst, a thunder to beat all thunders shook the world; and the monkey jumped.

Don Seráfico, deflated and spent, managed to catch sight of him. Bathed in tears, he whimpered: "He's a little ugly, but who cares?"

Window on Birth

The pregnant woman knows when and who. She knows when by what the moon and her body tell her. She knows who by what her dreams say. If she dreams about thread or bowls, she will have a daughter. If she dreams about metal, hats, or eggs, she will have a son.

Then she squats, lets down her hair, takes a swallow of liquor, and on her knees she gives birth.

The little hands of the baby touch a hoe, an axe, and a machete. With soot from the kitchen the mother marks the center of its head.

The umbilical cord is left at the tip of the highest tree.

This is how birth takes place in Chamula.

Story of the Overly Endowed, His Feats, and His Astonishing Fate

The curious crouched down in the hills to spy on him from afar. Encarnación had a huge head with ears that stuck out like fans and fiery hair, but from a distance all that could be seen was his stinger, which he dragged behind him like a long tail: on hot days Encarnación would bathe it in the river, then set it out on shore to dry in the sun, and on cold nights he used it as a scarf.

People said that hideous instrument was the result of the forbidden passion between a father and his daughter, and they said he used it to knock on doors, to bang in poles, and to try to satisfy his incessant lust. When he was in heat in the spring, Encarnación sat

as many as six women at once on his stiff crossbar, and played seesaw with them. And one night while he slept, the lewd monster had an erotic dream, and his mast rose up and drilled a hole through the tiles of the roof.

People said, people knew. No one, ever, had come close to him.

Night fell and a figure wandered sadly across the fields. Encarnación was walking alone as he always did, in one of those forever lonely solitudes, when a cloudburst took him by surprise.

Not one tree could be seen in the vastness.

Pelted by the rain, his teeth chattering from the cold, Encarnación caught sight of a bare rock that rose above the verdure. A bolt of lightning illuminated it: the boulder had a roof, and at its feet lay a porch and a corral.

The three sisters showed him in and bolted the door. One untied that thing around his neck, took off his soaking clothes, and wrapped him in a sheet. Another stirred up the fire and invited him to stretch out on a sheepskin on the hearth. The third brought to his lips *muña-muña* soup laced with hot peppers, cock's-comb tamales spread with virgin honey, and an omelette made of goat's balls fried in peanut oil. Encarnación drank hot corn wine mixed with ground deer's antlers, and he listened to the Bible of Jerusalem: the pious women recited for him the versicles which teach that better than wine are the kisses of your lips.

Outside, it was no longer raining.

Day broke on the mountainous horizon and the father of the maidens, who had come from afar on horseback, saw blood in the sky.

He dismounted, piled the things he'd bought in town on the porch, and looked over the stone wall of the corral. His daughters hadn't let out the animals. In the hen house, the hens were sleeping on their eggs and had no grain to eat.

Horrible foreboding. The father rounded up his far-off neighbors. An army, machetes bristling, marched uphill toward the house on the bluff.

Silence.

The father kicked open the door.

No one heard the crash, no one was awakened by the violent light of day. They were sleeping near the embers, naked under the sheets, and without even a blink they went on sleeping. The satyr, also asleep, also naked, was hanging from the roof, swinging softly, with his serpent tied to a rafter.

The father stampeded. Machete in hand, he jumped at the fearful creature that had disgraced his daughters. But before steel touched him, Encarnación dissolved in a puff of smoke and became nothing more than a handful of sulfur dust on the dirt floor.

At the thanksgiving mass, the priest celebrated the end of the nightmare of all good Christians. Encarnación had been a dream of the Devil, and he had vanished in the air when the Devil awoke.

The rainy season passed, and the dry season as well, the time of mud and the time of dust. And in the Paute River valley three children were born, with enormous red heads and the bodies of spiders. Each of them had an incredibly long appendage, which the midwife confused with the umbilical cord.

Window on Fear

Hunger breakfasts on fear. The fear of silence rattles the streets.
Fear threatens:

    If you love, you get AIDS.

    If you smoke, you get cancer.

    If you breathe, you get polluted.

    If you drink, you get accidents.

    If you eat, you get cholesterol.

    If you speak up, you get fired.

    If you walk, you get mugged.

    If you think, you get worried.

    If you doubt, you get crazy.

    If you feel, you get lonely.

Story of the Treasure That Was Discovered and How Its Curse Was Fulfilled

Under a punishing sun, the chronicler navigates the Caroní River in search of the treasure hunter.

When he finds him, he offers him a meal and receives a story in return.

Don Espíritu Morales kisses the cup and the rum disappears. He pours himself another and toasts: "For the pretext."

The platter of corn delights—tender corn wrapped in goat's cheese, mature corn embracing ham—evaporates in the twinkling of an eye.

"Do you smoke?" Don Espíritu asks. It is his way of asking for tobacco.

In the family restaurant El Buen Gusto, in the shade of a stick-and-palmleaf roof, the chronicler waits. He nibbles on something, takes a sip or two, and waits. The chicken stew has arrived, steaming,

juicy, smelling of coriander, and Don Espíritu dives into the blue-edged white porcelain bowl.

Once the stew is gone, and before the fish fried in garlic fills Don Espíritu's mouth, the chronicler receives his first words. And he learns that the treasure contained the fortunes of twenty-eight temples. The year was 1817, a time of rebellion, a time of pillage, and more than fifty mules carried the gold and jewels from the churches to the convent of the Catalonian missionary fathers in San Serafín. And there, in a secret place, the priest Inocencio buried the treasure of all treasures.

"One night on a binge, far from here, I found out. A grandson of the friar's grandson told me. And don't kid yourself, I didn't get it for free."

The grandson of the grandson demanded twenty-eight percent, and to Don Espíritu that seemed fair.

And the fish arrives.

And afterward: "Do you smoke?"

Don Espíritu takes a few puffs and chases them with a glass of rum.

And he talks. A fisherman took him to the ruins of the mission. Nobody was there. The ghost of Father Inocencio lived in a ceiba tree, and people were terrified of him. The fisherman knew the only person who could speak to the dead man.

"To give me the name he asked for ten percent. That seemed fair."

The goat's turn. A dish of goat in coconut milk. Don Espíritu didn't leave a speck. And of the trimmings, not even a grain of rice.

"Don Machuca de Guasipati," he continued, "understood the friar word for word. He told me not to bring a knife or a revolver because the phantom was the jittery type. And off we went."

Don Espíritu casts an imploring glance toward the kitchen. The chronicler nods, calming him, and serves more rum.

And the protagonist startles a few flies, adjusts his chair: "You know what? Don Machuca charged twenty-five percent."

And he explains, trying to convince or to convince himself: "There was no other interpreter."

And he concludes: "It seemed fair."

At midnight, the specter gave testimony.

A light flickered amid the branches of the immense tree. It left the leafy treetop and came bounding down. The intruders leapt back. Then the light stopped short, retreated, and hid in the tree.

Peeking over the shoulder of Don Espíritu, whom he used like a shield, Don Machuca begged: "Please stay, father."

And soon a tall white shape leaned against the trunk and remarked: "I might."

Friar Inocencio spoke in a voice worn out from being dead so long, but it sounded quite natural.

Don Machuca made the proposal.

"I might," said the grounded light.

Don Machuca wanted to pin it down, and the priest repeated: "I might."

Still crouched behind his client, Don Machuca whispered: "Make an offer."

And Don Espíritu offered: "For your redemption, sad suffering soul, I offer seven masses with requiescats, fourteen shrouds, and twenty-one rosaries which I shall pray every day until peace returns to your soul."

Then the light flashed and disappeared. In vain Don Espíritu banged on the trunk of the ceiba with his knuckles: "Father Inocencio, are you there?"

By now new steaming platters had begun the trip to the table, but Don Espíritu manages to get the story out. One night after many comings and goings, the phantom reappeared and with white fingers drew some vaporous signs in the darkness. Don Machuca translated: the priest demanded fifty percent of all the income derived from the buried goods, free of taxes and cleansed of all dust and straw. In the end he settled for forty percent.

"And did you think that was fair?" the chronicler asks.

The treasure hunter leaves a spoonful of fat red beans suspended in the air: "Don't kid me. Have you ever bargained with the dead?"

And Don Espíritu digs into a juicy tangle of shredded beef bathed in tomatoes, peppers, and egg, while a fresh bottle of rum lands amid the dishes.

At the appointed hour, they crossed the pit where the bones of the convent priests lay. When the phantom moved there was no sound of dragging chains. He fairly flew.

"Follow me, son," he ordered, raising a torch of pitch, and all four followed him: the grandson of his grandson, the fisherman, Don Machuca, and Don Espíritu.

Father Inocencio, who to hide his age was wearing a wig that belonged to the Carmelite Virgin, passed though the walls as if they were mist, opening them to the entire retinue.

They went straight to the back of the ruined convent, then down into its depths. And at a dead end, in the only place not soaked by the sweating rocks, the friar said: "Here."

At the exhumation, all were present.

Watching.

No one helped. Don Espíritu shouldered the excavation all by himself. And when he was in over his head, his shovel broke on the chest.

There were no jewels. The chest was filled with coins: gold onzas, rupees, piasters, doubloons. There were talents from the Aegean Sea and drachmas from Persia, Ptolemaic coins from the pharaohs of Egypt and dirhams from the caliphs of Cordova, libras from Sicily and denarii from Rome, florins from Florence, ducats from Aragon, maravedis from Castile.

Don Espíritu chews golden coins made of mashed plantain.

"Do you know how much I got? This," he says, and a small effigy emerges from his ragged clothing.

"Nobody wanted it," he says.

The chronicler picks it up, looks at it, and it looks at the chronicler: a female saint carved in jacaranda wood, worm-eaten and ugly, without eyes yet somehow staring.

"Ah!" sighs the discoverer of treasures, smiling from ear to ear: the fried plate has arrived, dripping delights.

"I don't get it," the chronicler says, "if you'll excuse me."

Don Espíritu sucks his teeth, concentrating on his own pleasure.

"So much work, and for what? I don't get it."

Don Espíritu wields a pork rib, points at the chronicler's chest: "But listen, kid," he says. And he goes on eating. And the chronicler remains silent.

A good while later, Don Espíritu raises up a drumstick: "I looked for the treasure," he says. "And I found it. Me."

"Yeah. And what did you get out of it?"

The discoverer licks his fingers and says: "Once you've got it, you've got it."

The whole region saluted him. He shook so many hands that his own became rough and edgy like an old knife.

But the feast didn't last long. The triumphant treasure hunter went on living in utter misery, scraping by on handouts. The Commission of Ladies for the Betterment of Caroní River and the Society for the Protection of Animals and the Poor soon publicly repudiated him for his greed, and the Holy Father in Rome sued him for rob-

bery. And the suspicion quickly spread throughout the entire region that this multimillionaire had once again buried the chest brimming with treasure, who knows where.

A stray dog scratches his back in the doorway of the restaurant and comes over to lie near the table.

Don Espíritu accepts the tray of fruit. His knife denudes a ripe pineapple.

"Another thing I don't understand," the chronicler insists. "Why didn't they get it themselves?"

And then he risks two fingers and snatches a grape from the tray Don Espíritu protects with his arms.

"They, I mean. They knew. Why did they wait so long? Why did you have to come along?"

Don Espíritu scratches his several-days beard growing on a cheek distended with fruit.

"Pinheads."

And he finishes swallowing, and shaking his head he says: "They believed in the curse."

He tackles the medlar, spits out a few seeds.

"To dig up the treasure would bring misfortune. That's what they believed."

And he laughs and laughs, and coughing he proclaims: "Look, some people are superstitious, right?"

The chronicler wants to smoke, but Don Espíritu is puffing away on his last cigarette.

A mosquito torments the chronicler's ear and sticks him with its lance.

Somebody's whistling.

With his gaze, the dog on the floor follows the travels: that of the smoke, that of the mosquito, that of the whistle.

Window on Inheritance

Pola Bonilla modeled clay and children. She was a potter of steady hand and a schoolteacher in the fields of Maldonado; and in the summers she sold her trinkets and hot chocolate with churros to the tourists.

Pola adopted a black baby born in poverty, one of many who arrive in the world without a loaf of bread under their arms, and she raised him as her son.

When she died, he was a grown man with a trade. Pola's relatives said to him: "Go into the house and take whatever you want."

He came out with her picture under his arm and was lost from sight down the road.

Story of the Redemption of Poverty

The last rooster was already soup. His widows scratched the earth in search of grain, and they found garbage.

The town was on its last legs. There was not a single coin to pay the merchants who once in a great while passed through. In payment they took the only things there were: the women were left with their heads shorn and the men with only one kidney.

In the middle of the night, Felicindo went fishing for something to ease his hunger. He was on his way to the river when all of a sudden the brush jumped up and trapped him. Thorny tentacles blocked his way and launched the attack. Felicindo defended himself by swinging his machete, but the severed branches fused anew and the weeds he tossed back rose up again. The brush had begun to eat him when suddenly tongues of fire opened a path in the thicket.

The blaze split the woods in two and surged, unstoppable, toward the horizon. There, far off, it turned into a rainbow. Motionless amid the fallen brambles, Felicindo saw the rainbow display its long colorful tail across the blackness of the sky, and he fainted.

The next night, Felicindo was walking toward the Cirrhosis bar, which had once been a tortilla shop called The Alchemist in the remote days when the town still ate, when a stranger emerged from the ravine and started walking at his side.

The man glowed, a brilliance never beheld: his gear was pure gold, and an enormous charro's hat brimming with diamonds covered his face. He walked without seeing, but with a steady gait; and despite the darkness Felicindo could tell that one foot had a boot and spur, and the other was a horse's skull.

No words passed between them. Halfway there, the traveler stopped to smoke. He didn't offer, and Felicindo was struck by his manner: the man pulled a silver dollar from his ear and with his thumbnail struck a flame. When he lit the cigarette, his attire glowed like embers, from the lonely boot
to the jewel-studded Jalisco hat.

Felicindo was going to ask him for a small loan, but at that very moment a rooster crowed from one of the houses. It was the town's last rooster, the sacrificial rooster, crowing from the dead; he crowed at the wrong times, for the pleasure of being a pest. And just as the cock-a-doodle-doo broke open the night, the elegant gentleman vanished into the brush, tossing off flames amid the foliage.

Then some time went by without a visit. In vain Felicindo wandered the thickets in search of a trace of sparks in the air. He couldn't sleep, he couldn't fish, he couldn't do anything: the damned fire had stolen his stride.

When the glow returned, it was a female glow, a señora who radiated black light from the top of a hill. Covering herself with a black silk parasol, she blocked the cold rays of the moon, and a black lace veil hid her face. The breeze raised it slightly and she offered her lips. And Felicindo kissed.

"Thank you," said the lady of the night, in a hoarse voice, her throat punished from hard living, and she repeated: "Thank you."

That sandpaper voice broke with emotion. The Devil was a poor devil condemned to scaring people, and Felicindo was the only poor human who had neither been frightened, nor insulted him, nor denounced him, nor offered his soul in exchange for power or wealth.

"I have come to bring you a gift," the raspy voice announced from behind the black veil. It was the secret for escaping misery.

"There is a different sort of life someplace," she whispered in his ear, "and that place is here."

"I'm poor," said Felicindo.

"No, compadre. Fortune surrounds you."

Her black gloves took it all in: "Tell me, compadre. What do you see?"

Felicindo looked around him. The drought, the gravelly earth.

"Stones," he said.

The next day, Felicindo filled a bag with stones, slung it over his shoulder, and set off toward the city of Oaxaca.

He walked for several days, bent over from the weight. And in a market on the outskirts, sitting on the ground, he called out his wares. From dawn onward, Felicindo wore himself out shouting: "Stones! Stones!"

No one bought.

When night fell, he gave up. He collected his stones, and with them over his shoulder and his soul in his feet, he left the market, which by now was empty.

And he started back. The night was freezing and Felicindo shivered from cold and loneliness. At the edge of the city he came across a heap in the middle of the road. It was an old woman wrapped in her shawl, eating tortillas, indifferent to the automobiles that nearly brushed against her. By the light of the moon, all he could see was the working of her mouth. The old woman offered Felicindo a few tortillas, and gave him a mask to shelter him: "Cover up your face, it's the most naked."

And a masked Felicindo went on, until after a lot of walking across the countryside, he saw fire amid some rocks at the back of a hill. And he put his sack on the ground and there, near the flames, he collapsed into sleep.

Felicindo didn't see that other men were sleeping in the warmth. They woke up before he did, with the first light, and when they saw him they howled "The Devil!" and shot off toward the horizon.

The shouting made him jump. Felicindo saw men flying off in a cloud of dust, and in a nearby pasture he saw a few mules grazing.

Abandoned in the mules' packs were the gold bars from the bank the thieves had held up.

Felicindo arrived back in town in a glorious procession. The mules led the caravan of fortune.

But there was no one left. Everyone had fled in terror and even Felicindo's wife, who was known to be a scoundrel and a rascal of a lady, let out a scream when she saw him and ran to find a crucifix.

Felicindo tried to rip off the mask with his fingernails, and he tried water and liquor, detergent and steel wool.

And to this day he wants to pull off the mask that the mirror shows him every morning.

He consoles himself with the knowledge that nearly everybody in the world has the same problem.

Window on Masks

El Ñato García pretended to be crazy in Australia.

It was late afternoon, he was watching the sun go down over Melbourne while in Montevideo it was coming up, and he decided to go crazy.

He had deliria and hallucinations. He fought against invisible enemies, throwing punches in the air, and he spent days and nights sitting against a wall without closing his eyes. He refused to speak because the demon of madness got in through his open mouth. He refused to sleep for fear of dying of madness during the night. He put up with pills, injections, electric shocks. And at last, after four years of refusing to allow himself even a shadow of normality, the doctors of Australia became convinced that he was an incurable case.

Thus El Ñato got a ticket home and a good pension on which he could live without working for the rest of his life. One last time he looked in the mirror in his home in Melbourne, he said goodbye to the crazy man, and got on the plane.

And he arrived in the city of his nostalgia.

In Montevideo he looked. He looked for his childhood home and in its place was a supermarket. The empty field where he'd made love the first time was a parking lot. He looked for his friends. They were gone. He looked and he looked, and nowhere could he find himself, and that's when a doubt entered his mind: "Who was it that stayed back there in Melbourne? The crazy man or me?"

Once a year, only once, El Ñato recognizes himself in the mirror. Carnival time comes with its thunderous drums and El Ñato recognizes himself. That happens when the mirror shows him a busker: clown nose, big smile painted over his lips, the moon between his eyebrows, and stars strewn all over his face.

Story of the Art of Flight

"Look, Primero."

"Speak, Segunda."

She handed him the binoculars. From high up on the lookout, the lord of Tucumán spied a misshapen insect that seemed lost on the vast red expanse. The insect grew, and the binoculars soon revealed a little man who approached, misbegetting misfortune.

And then Don Primero discovered that his daughter Dolores was standing below, in the middle of the valley, awaiting the misbegetter.

Cantalicio Galante had come on foot, angling across from the blue sierra. He did not take off his sombrero, nor did he toss the old cigarette butt that hung off his lips. Dolores looked him in the face. Not he, because she was so pretty his eyes hurt to look at her. Cantalicio stared at the ground, but under his eyelashes his gaze slid to the side and scanned the length of the woman's shadow, it found her ankles and, dying to see more, climbed the legs that the breeze outlined under the linen skirt.

They did not touch, even with words.

Don Primero laughed with fury, slapped the side of his head, and roared out threats against that brash lad, useless scrap, man's tit; but he didn't kill him. The law would have allowed it, a law he himself had decreed; but he didn't kill him. He demanded three tasks.

Don Primero ordered him to stuff a pillow with frog feathers. From his chair Cantalicio murmured: "A frog with feathers has never been seen."

But Dolores set off for the lake where the fifty frogs from the far-off Parapetí River lived.

At that river, a frog had challenged an ostrich to a race. After a few strides the ostrich left his rival far behind. He looked back to see

him, but the frog was leaping along far ahead. This happened fifty times in that endless race: the ostrich looked for the frog way behind and found him way ahead. In the end the exhausted ostrich paid for his defeat by denuding himself and handing over all his feathers. And the fifty winners, who one after the other had taken over the race, stayed on to live in the lake where Dolores went. She told them the sorrows of her love life, and the frogs gave her their trophy.

Cantalicio delivered the pillow he had stuffed to order with the frogs' feathers. Then Don Primero demanded a jug of birds' tears.

And Cantalicio murmured, his face to the ground: "A bird that cries has never been seen."

Seated at his side, her face upturned, Dolores was off in the clouds. On the fields of the sky galloped horses with manes of women's hair and tails of serpents; on the sea above drifted ships with sails and flags.

Suddenly Dolores jumped up and pointed to a cloud that flew slowly with outspread wings.

When the cloud cried tears of rain, she filled the jug.

Cantalicio rubbed a sword with a rag. It was the final test. Don Primero had ordered that by midnight the sword had to be clean, but the bloodstain kept coming back. Each time the rag wiped it clean, the blade of steel sweated more blood.

"With that sword he'll kill you," warned Dolores, and before midnight the two of them fled. She dug seven holes in the floor of her bedroom and spit in each one, then left, taking with her a pair of scissors, a fistful of ashes, a handful of salt, a comb, and a mirror.

Seven times Don Primero asked: "Are you there?"
  And seven times the saliva answered: "I'm here."
  The eighth time the father flung open the door.

He pursued them mounted on a black sow.
  The sow hurtled straight toward them, and the fugitives saw her
coming, spouting water and thunder by the light of the moon that

gave them away. Then Dolores threw the scissors, which fell point down on the road. Where they fell, a wall of sharp-peaked mountains rose up.

The thunderous noise of pursuit woke them at dawn. When the sow emerged from the mountains at full gallop, Dolores threw the fistful of ashes into the air and the new day was masked in darkness. Under a curtain of mist, they slipped away.

Dolores ran, dragging along her bowlegged lover; but every few steps Cantalicio tripped and fell down on the grass, wanting to kiss and smoke and take a nap under his sombrero.

And once again they heard the approaching din. The sow and her rider, a roaring whirlwind, charged blindly at the fallen figure. And then Dolores threw the handful of salt and a deluge of hail halted the stampede.

Cantalicio was on his last legs. Battered, out of breath, he could not go on. By then the intrepid and gallant young man was ready to return Don Primero's most prized possession, and in his mind he was preparing a speech that invoked national reconciliation and sent aloft doves of peace and made the stones cry. But Dolores picked him up, shook him, pushed him forward and proclaimed that it was better to die together than to survive as halves.

When the sow attacked again, a hurtling cannonball, Dolores threw the comb. A jungle of branches sprouted forth and in a flash it bisected the world from horizon to horizon.

The sow took a long time to eat her way through that dense thicket. When the last twig was gone, she shot off once more, shrieking with thirst, the wind whistling under her belly and Don Primero hanging off her back. Then Dolores threw the mirror and a lake as big as the sea opened out of the earth.

In vain Don Primero dug in his spurs and spit out damnations. The sow was wetting her whistle and no longer had the slightest interest in punishing the delinquents, who were lost from sight.

Doña Eva, Cantalicio's mother, was not surprised that Dolores had chased after him from so far away. She knew no woman in the world was worthy of her treasure. And to make her point she left a broom lying across the vestibule.

But Dolores not only stepped over the broom, she grabbed it and swept the house. And not only the house: she swept the neighborhood and the entire town and the next town over and the whole region.

The priest married them. There was a fiesta, with plenty of drink and food and offerings of honey and wine and Scott's Emulsion.

And if the town had had a newspaper, it would have reported that after a pleasant courtship, Dolores Primero and Cantalicio Galante became a happy couple, uniting their young lives forever in a solemn ceremony that sealed their destinies before the All-Powerful, until death do them part.

The next day Cantalicio made a little boat from a paper napkin and let himself float away.

Dolores caught it just as he was drifting down the ditch, headed for the river.

Window on Luck

At midnight on the eve of Saint John's day, fires burn on the shores of the island of Puerto Rico.

That night people throw themselves into the water backwards to ward off misfortune and bad vibes. And eligible women eat a boiled egg with lots of salt at bedtime, so someone will bring them fresh water in their dreams.

During the night of Saint John's, fig trees, mint, and bamboo all flower, and at dawn people go in search of these good omens.

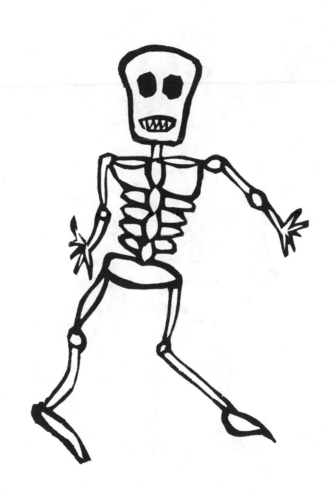

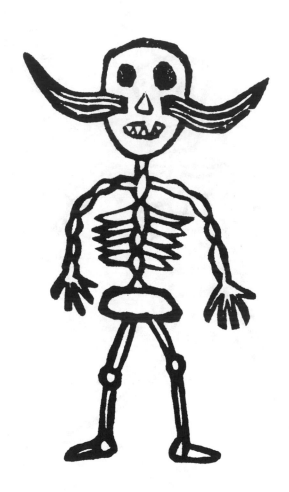

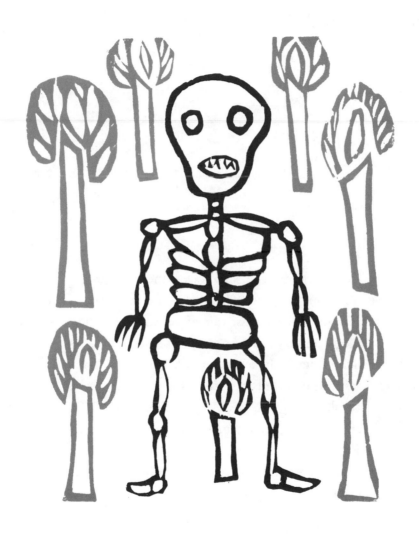

Story of Don Death, the Sad Girl, and the Vulture

She had lost her soul and could not find it anywhere. Mora had stopped wanting to live, and those who understood shrugged their shoulders: "There's no cure for love."

The woman sang her broken song for no one.

Three times she sang it. The third time an echo answered her sorrowful refrain. The response came from the other shore, and Mora crossed the Huichihuayan River at the stone crossing.

Every inch of her body ached, even her hair, but she pursued the lament that echoed, faded into the distance, and was lost. She pursued it, stumbling by the weak light of the moon, from knoll to knoll, league after league, accompanied only by the owls that circled over the hilltops.

At long last she found the voice where her voice went. And she entered the darkness.

The talking skeleton welcomed her: "This is your home."

Deep within the cave, candles shone. Thousands upon thousands of candles of all sizes and colors: there were long wax tapers with nascent flames, and huge vigil lights burning brightly, and piles of candles without much wick that dripped streams of cold and colorless wax.

The candles, bodies aflame, bristled on the walls the entire length of the cavern, and shadows glowed on the ceiling. The entire province of Huehuetlán was present in that radiance. No one was missing: there lay the poor and the rich, the fresh and the tired, the nude and the disguised.

"Underground there are no crowns," said the skeleton. "Neither of gold nor of thorns."

He bowed and introduced himself: "The Leveler. The Bald One. The Chatterer. The Stinker. The Rasper. The Toothy One. The Trembler. The Duster. The Blackened One."

And in a gooey, wheedling voice, he clarified: "They give me women's names. Don't believe it."

Every few steps, the owner of the fires stopped and blew. He blew in all directions and snuffed out flames for good. Pointing to a tall red candle that kept sputtering on and off, he asked: "That doubtful fire, do you recognize it?"

Mora's blood ran cold.

She'd never forgotten him. She saw him once in her childhood, in a procession. Mora was the Little Virgin of Guadalupe on a throne of flowers, naked under the white gauze, her eyes upturned, her hands clasped, and the skeleton suddenly emerged from among the palm leaves on the altar. He winked at her and the girl fell to the floor.

And now her own legs had carried her to the lugubrious kingdom, and she could not bear to listen to the screeching of that jaw.

The marzipan skull let loose an operatic cackle and moved away. He detested being rushed in such ghastly affairs.

Days went by.

Mora remained a prisoner. An obsequious Don Death tempted her with sugar teeth, chocolate whiskers: he offered an end to all pain, the kiss to erase all the kisses ever kissed or to be kissed, the move-no-more, the always-never. While he whispered in her ear, his bony hands wove long garlands of black flowers and carved and polished an obsidian cross in the form of a woman's body.

Mora was afraid to look at herself in the cave's puddle, her only mirror, because the puddle might drink her face.

Don Death sent Mora on a trip around the moor. And he ordered her to dig a grave with her fingernails in the spot with the best earth and the best shade.

Then Mora tried to flee. The moment the thought crossed her mind, the earth split with a colossal crack and a precipice opened at her feet.

Mora cried, she cried for herself.

But then the wind blew, the wind that blows anywhere, and the condemned woman felt the astonishment of having been born and the curiosity of living. Of living whatever way she could, in whatever place, for whatever length of time: the hours of the butterfly, the days of the fly, the centuries of the tortoise.

And she screamed. And the great white-breasted vulture heard her from the heights, and flew down and landed at her side.

And Mora received the vulture's feathers in exchange for her hair, and his wings in exchange for her arms.

She was afraid. She was terrified of the depths that lay before her. She backed up to get a running start, took a few steps, and at the edge of the abyss fell back. That's what she was doing, yes then no, when the vulture gave her a shove and in the midst of falling she spread her wings and the wings sustained her as she drifted in the lightness of free air. And her joy was so great that she envied herself.

Memory eats the dead. The vulture, too. Just like memory, the vulture flies.

And that vulture, who out of habit ate the dead and converted them into the strength of his wings, went happily into the cavern where the songs of irremediable sorrow found their destiny.

Don Death saw the bulk coming, woman's hair, woman's shadow swaggering alongside the tapers, and he jumped on it.

But the vulture kissed first. He buried his powerful beak in the mouth of death and bit and ate. Tears came to his eyes, because death, which seemed sweet, was burning hot, hotter than habanero chilies or the angry peppers of the Devil's garden.

Window on Mirrors

The sun shines and carries away the shadowy remains of night.

Horse-drawn carriages pick up the garbage, door to door.

In the air the spider spins its threads of saliva.

El Tornillo walks the streets of Melo. People in town think he's crazy. He carries a mirror in his hand and he looks at himself with furrowed brow. He doesn't take his eyes off the mirror.

"What are you doing, Tornillo?"

"I'm here," he says, "keeping watch on the enemy."

Window on Death (I)

Helena Villagra couldn't open her eyes. They burned. She rubbed them and her eyelashes fell out, her eyebrows too. She was at the movies. When at last she managed to see, she saw a black screen.

Window on Death (II)

Alberto's ashes were already lying in the earth of Tucumán. Alberto's ashes were already growing in the verdure of that place.

Helena inherited his hat. Helena would sleep and Alberto's hat slept too. And in Helena's dream, the hat would dream.

The hat dreamt that it flapped its wings and spun around to take off with Helena inside, curled up in the crown.

She woke up seasick from so much spinning.

Story of the Cowboy Who Was a Jaguar

He was a man of powers and mysteries. It was something you wouldn't believe. His gaze opened wounds or closed them, and made beasts and humans faint or revive. One clap of his eyes would knock silly the wildest bronco or the bulliest bull.

Ventura, the wandering cowboy of Minas Gerais, passed through like the wind. He had many routes, many women; he had no home.

He had only one friend, and the two of them were halters made from the same rope.

They were wandering in the dustbowl. They hadn't eaten a thing in several days. In pursuit of some hopeless cause they had lost their horses and their way. Nothing to eat: lizards, thorns, brush with neither fruit nor shade. Ventura was used to it, but his friend could not go on. And when the friend lay down to die in the midst of all that solitude, Ventura transformed himself into a jaguar to save him from starvation.

Before he turned into a jaguar, he gave his friend a blue leaf with points like a star, not from any known tree, and he said: "When I come back, put this leaf on my tongue."

And he said there was no other way to disenjag himself.

He traveled far, spent the night hunting.

He returned at dawn, with the first white light, carrying a deer on his back. When the friend saw him coming, when he saw that huge jaguar coming at him with his jaws wide, he fled in terror.

The jaguar watched him run. He didn't give chase.

Wherever he went, he left nothing alive. He broke open stones, flattened hills, made ravines collapse. Lying in the tall grass, the jaguar raised his head and sniffed the wind and roared in sad rage; and no one slept.

The hunt was long. An army of vultures following his footprints alerted the army of men on his trail.

And the noose tightened, a galloping circle of sweat and clatter, thunder of shots and cries and barks, until one moonlit night the jaguar leapt for the last time, high into the air, and he roared and fell. He was already dead from the rain of bullets when Ventura's friend thrust his rifle barrel down the jaguar's throat and pulled the trigger.

Far from there, Ventura awoke. He was smeared with dried blood and tormented by aches and pains from his hat to his feet.

Even breathing was painful. Walking was very hard, enormous staggering shadow, and remembering was very hard. When? Where? Who? High moon, evil moon. Night had fallen, inside him night

had fallen, and night was no longer the time for love or war. His eyes had gone mute, and he only had ears for the drip-drip-drip of death. Fucking life, life without a spark. Reviving? Redying. Ashes waiting to be blown out by God.

White from dust, black from dirt, red from blood, Ventura comes up the alley. Burdened by pain, he drags his feet. His legs can barely hold up that enormous ruin of a body.

Ventura crosses the market, deaf to the clamor of the market women, and, squinting, he makes out ahead, at the end of every-

thing, the saloon. Its limestone facade shines brightly at the foot of the dragon's crest of hills, and even closer shines the sweat of the horses tied up to the posts.

At the entrance a blind man sings the news. The mouth of the blind man sings what his ears have seen, while a tin can of change marks the beat. The blind man sings ballads about the horrible jaguar, scourge of the fields, who caused so many deaths and died killing.

With a trembling hand, Ventura raises the broken brim of his hat, wipes the sweat that clouds his sight and sees: he sees the skin of the jaguar hanging from a wire in the sun to dry. More holes than you could count. The bullets hadn't left much for the moths.

And he enters the saloon.

The friend sees him coming, sees that bag of bones coming, and the glass of cane liquor slips from his fingers and crashes to the floor.

Everyone shuts up, everything.

PEDRA

CAÇADOR DE ONÇ

Pedra

A J. BORGES

Window on Mistakes

It happened in the time of long nights and icy winds: one morning the jasmine flowered in my garden, and the cold air was impregnated with the fragrance, and on that day the plum tree also flowered and the turtles awoke.

It was a mistake and did not last. But thanks to that mistake, the jasmine, the plum tree, and the turtles could believe that some day winter would end. Me too.

Story of the Bird That Lost a Leg

Her children had already broken through the eggs and were shrieking in the nest. Tenquita flew off to find food for them. It was winter in Colchagua and the snow froze one of her legs. The bird protested: "Why did you make me lame?"

And the snow said, "Because the sun melts me."

And Tenquita complained to the sun, and the sun said: "Because the mist covers me."

And the mist: "Because the wind blows me."

And the wind: "Because the wall blocks me."

And the wall: "Because the mouse makes holes in me."

And the mouse: "Because the cat eats me."

And the cat: "Because the dog chases me."

And the dog: "Because the stick beats me."

And the stick: "Because the fire burns me."

And the fire: "Because the water quenches me."

And the water: "Because the cow drinks me."

And the cow: "Because the knife kills me."

And the knife: "Because the man sharpens me."

And the man: "Because God made me."

Stumbling as she walked, Tenquita sang for God. And God heard her, and then she asked him why he had made the man that sharpens the knife that kills the cow that drinks the water that quenches the fire that burns the stick that beats the dog that chases the cat that eats the mouse that makes holes in the wall that blocks the wind that blows the mist that covers the sun that melts the snow that froze my leg.

"Oh, Tenquita," God said. "I had to make man so man could make me."

Window on the Word (V)

Javier Villafañe searches in vain for the word that slipped away just as he was about to say it. It was right on the tip of his tongue. Where did it go?

Is there a place for all the words that don't want to stay? A kingdom of lost words? These words that escape, where do they lie in wait?

Story of the Divine Revelation of a Dog's Life in This World

"Do you mind?"

"We like the company."

"Thanks very much."

"My name's Flores. Profession: guitarist, at your service."

"Charmed. Ceniza. Profession: dog."

"Would you like a maté?"

"I don't usually."

"What a coincidence. I was just remembering that old tune about tails."

"Which one?"

" 'The pain a dog feels when they cut off his tail . . .' "

"Oh, yeah. I know it: '. . . is like what the tail feels when they cut off the dog.' "

"That's the one."

"The fact is, Don Flores, we don't know much about tails."

"Not much. We know there was a fiesta in heaven. You dogs took a dip in a river, not the Paraná, but a river up there in Paradise . . ."

"And we left our tails to dry on the bank. A wet tail won't chase mosquitos."

"Right. All the tails on the bank, in a line."

"And God played that trick on us. He made the river rise."

"The river flooded."

"And we had to get out of there in a hurry. In the rush, everybody grabbed the first tail he found. Since then we've been sniffing each other to find the one we lost."

"Everybody knows that story, Don Ceniza."

"People believe it, and so do we."

"It's well known."

"But it didn't happen."

"Who says it didn't happen?"

"God."

"Oh."

"The Great Canine."

"What, did you see him?"

"Whoever sees him goes blind. I felt him. I had my back turned and I felt something sacred."

"Our god doesn't appear often."

"Neither does ours."

"And he chose you."

"This humble servant."

"You're lucky."

"Don't believe it. God told me to spread the truth to the dogs of the world. He told me to say that that fiesta in heaven never happened."

"And did you spread the word?"

"That we have no tail to seek? I kept quiet."

"I think I see, Don Ceniza."

"Yes, Don Flores."

"The reason for your silence."

"Now no path beckons to me."

"Right."

"Before I was footloose and fancy free. I went everywhere. In those days no tail belonged to me."

"And now . . ."

"Now it seems like I'm going, but I'm coming."

"A dog's luck."

"A dog's world."

"Fate."

"Don Flores?"

"What?"

"Keep my secret."

"You can trust me."

"And watch out for the cold, Don Flores. Your throat."

Window on Art (I)

In Zaragoza they paid homage to the ruins of a beautiful Moorish tower. They didn't build another to evoke the tower that once was: instead a bronze child sits hugging his knees and looks at the huge hole where it stood.

Window on Art (II)

I was a boy, practically a child, and I wanted to draw. By lying about my age, I snuck in with the students who were sketching a nude.

In the classes, I kept wasting paper struggling to find lines and shapes. That naked woman, who shifted her pose, was a challenge for my clumsy hand and nothing more: something like a breathing vase.

But one night at the bus stop, I saw her dressed for the first time. When she stepped into the bus, her skirt slid up and revealed the threshold of her thigh. That was when my body burned.

Window on the Word (VI)

The A has its legs spread wide.

The M is a seesaw that rides up and down between heaven and hell.

The O, a closed circle, suffocates you.

The R is notoriously pregnant.

"All the letters of the word AMOR are dangerous," Romy Díaz-Perera says.

When words come out of her mouth, she sees them drawn in the air.

Story of the Dolphin That Satan Caught without a Harpoon or a Lure

The full moon lit up the waters of the Amazon. A dolphin leapt nimbly into the air, doing circus tricks amid the resplendent waves. There was a big to-do in one town, a lot of carrying on and dancing, and the cries of the music lovers called to the dolphin from the coast.

And for the first time, the moon, who had never paid him any heed, said all right: that night, as long as the night lasted, he would be allowed to go on dry land.

The dolphin stood tall and naked on the sand, and the moon gave him a new body and new clothes.

He went to the fiesta.

He danced with his hat on, so no one would see the breathing hole in his head. And he left the crowd with their mouths open: everyone was astonished by his reddish skin with blue glimmers and by the look from his widely spaced eyes, and by his thirst that liters upon

liters of pure cane liquor would not quench. And everyone marveled at how he danced without touching the ground, submerging himself in the music, swimming in its waters.

And as he was undulating in the music, he embraced a woman. And later the two of them continued dancing, without clothes and without anyone else, to music born from their embraces.

He was used to playing in the water, but never had he swum inside a woman.

There he was lying on her when he felt a little tap, tap-tap, that burned his back. He turned over and looked: a phosphorescent flame rose in the air and took on claws and horns and a beard. A very red fellow swayed and shone in the blackness: "Get up, intruder," he said.

The dolphin was confused and did not understand.

The new arrival was hoarse, even though a silk kerchief protected his throat from the cold air of the tropics. Pointing to the watch on his wrist, he growled: "Get back in the river you ugly beast, your time is up."

And the dolphin remembered what he had forgotten. The night would soon be over, and with it would end his time on dry land. He looked at the woman curled up at his side, her long black hair a tangle of seaweed, and the hoarse voice scraped against his ear: "She's not bad."

And the red one smiled, with lots of teeth: "A nice present. It had to be today. Good Friday, my day."

And he reached with his claw toward the body that throbbed to the rhythm of her dream. The dolphin struck out at him, and the blow struck the empty air. She felt a little breeze, blinked, and went back to sleep.

The net swayed softly: the net that still held them both.

The Devil, who tries out hell's torments in this world, whispered a riddle: "With whom will this woman sleep tomorrow?"

And he flickered and faded away in the darkness. The last of the darkness: the ashy fog of dawn had already begun to spread through the air.

Borrowed night, borrowed body.

He cursed the moon for all that the moon had given, and he cursed the sun for all that the sun was going to take away.

She murmured something in her sleep and he hugged her tightly against his body. He wanted to take her but he could not, and he wanted to stay but could not either.

The early morning breeze ripples the river.

A few steps from the edge, a dolphin is dying.

The sun rises, and from the sky it awakens the colors and aromas of the world.

Once there was a time that was the first time, and that was when the human being rose up and his four feet became two arms and two legs, and thanks to the legs the arms were free and could build better houses than treetops or occasional caves. And having stood up, women and men discovered that they could make love face to face and mouth to mouth, and they learned the joy of looking into each other's eyes during the embrace of their arms and the knotting of their legs.

Window on the Word (VII)

He had been in prison for over twenty years when he spotted her.

He waved to her from the window of his cell, and she waved back from the window of her house.

Later, he spoke to her with colored rags and with big letters. The letters spelled out words that she read with a spyglass. She answered with even larger letters, since he had no spyglass.

And thus their love grew.

Now Nela and the Negro Viña sit back to back. If one gets up, the other falls over.

They sell wine across from the ruins of the Punta Carretas prison, in Montevideo.

Story of the Man Who in the High Heavens Loved a Star and Was Abandoned by Her

There were robberies but no thieves in the Valley of Cuzco.

The robberies occurred at night in the field with the best potatoes. The owner kept watch all night with his eyes wide, but at some point he let his lids fall shut and in that instant the potatoes disappeared, leaving behind rows of freshly dug holes.

One night, the man dissembled. He lay down flat in the middle of the field and snored with one eye open. Hours went by and when it was nearly dawn, a violent brilliance made him leap up.

So much light blinded him, but he managed to grab one of the thieves with his bare hands. The rest fled in a burst of flame high

into the sky, and there they stayed, illuminating what remained of the night.

The imprisoned star promised to return all the potatoes, and she begged: "Don't make me live on the earth."

But he would not let her go. He covered her luminous nakedness with wool clothing and closed her up in his house.

Some time later they had a son who died at birth.

And one day at sunset, when he wasn't looking, the luminary escaped to the heavens.

Thanks to the condor, the man flew after her.

During the long trip, the man and the condor grew older and older, until by its end they were centuries old. But as soon as they arrived, they dove into the lake of time, and swam, and emerged young again.

Then the man started racing around through the resplendent fog of the Milky Way. And in that pilgrimage he recognized his star. And he begged her to let him stay.

They lived together in a hidden corner of the heavens.

At every sunset, she would go with her sisters to illuminate the night of the universe. And at every dawn she would return, bringing earthly food which she found by slipping into the granaries of the sun and the moon.

And thus it was, until it could be no more.

One morning the star did not come home, and the man wandered through the cold mist of the heavens, hungry and alone, crying out for her.

The condor took him back to earth, and on the earth he died of sorrow.

He was never able to tell the story. Not a word issued from his lips, which did not open even to eat. Perhaps because he had been starstruck, or perhaps because he knew that here on earth they would take his story to be an obvious lie or the hallucination of a poor mortal who thinks he's god sitting on the throne of night's kingdom.

As for her, the starologists are not in agreement. There are those who say she fell out of love, and others who say that there is no reason to call by that name what was only pity or curiosity.

Some maintain she kicked the man out because she didn't want to see him die. According to these specialists, stars don't understand our habit of living only for a while, and neither do they understand our crazy desire to climb up to heaven: stars know nothing of human dying, but they do know that there above the clouds people cannot be reborn in the children they have, or in the potatoes they plant, or in the loves they leave behind.

Others believe it was an obligatory goodbye. The sun and the moon had warned the star that she had better find another galaxy in which to live with the intruder. Thus, it could not go on: in every domestic quarrel, the man aged a hundred years and she was left in total darkness. It's true that later on, when the two of them forgave each other for the stupidity of hating each other, he recovered the century he'd lost and she increased in splendor. But the peace of the firmament could not bear such upheavals. And it was then, it seems, that the heavenly bosses decided to give up the potatoes they liked so much, and the road to earth was rubbed out forever.

The star regretted having obeyed the order that condemned her to solitude. That's what one scholar who has spent his life photographing shooting stars claims. He is certain, and he says he has proof: shooting stars are all alike because they are all one. That one light, errant and wet, is the star that once knew the danger and joy of a human embrace, who became frightened and fled, and was pursued and found. Ever since then, her mute body, which once sang for the man, knows that it was born to be two or none. And now it flies crazily about through the night, in search of the lost road to this world.

Window on a Woman (I)

That woman is a secret house.

In her corners, she keeps voices and hides ghosts.

On winter nights, she gives off smoke.

Whoever enters her, they say, never leaves.

I cross the deep moat that surrounds her. In that house I will be lodged. In her awaits the wine that will drink me. Very softly I knock at the door, and I wait.

Window on a Woman (II)

The other key won't turn in the street door.

The other voice, funny, out of tune, doesn't sing in the shower.

In the bathroom there is no trace of wet footsteps.

No warm fragrance comes from the kitchen.

A half-eaten apple, marked with other teeth, begins to rot on the table.

A half-smoked cigarette, ash of a dead worm, stains the edge of the ashtray.

I think I ought to shave. I think I ought to get dressed. I think I ought to.

Dirty water rains inside me.

Window on a Woman (III)

No one could kill that time, no one: not even ourselves. I mean: as long as you are, wherever you are, or as long as I am.

The calendar says that that time, that short time, no longer exists; but tonight my naked body is oozing with you.

Window on Music (I)

"Those who really know how to play the accordion can make it talk,"
Don Alejo Durán liked to say. "For them, man and accordion are
one."

Don Alejo was a cowboy and a troubadour, master of the lasso
and the arpeggio, chronicling balladeer of the Colombian coast. And
always for pleasure, never for work. When he wasn't in love, his
accordion fell silent.

Crying tunes weren't his thing. Frank and joyful was his music,
and frank and joyful were the women his music called from afar,
with no need for a telephone.

Window on Music (II)

Papá Montero was a dance-man and crooner, the man who brought joy to the Havana night. The whole city danced the rumba with him, in him, and in his rumba let loose.

When a knife did in Papá Montero, the Havana night went mute. But in the middle of the wake a rumba was heard. Far off. Barely anyone noticed.

At dawn, when his friends went to carry the casket away, they found it empty.

Story of the Moon People

Old bones, eyes of no light. All yellow, it looks. I look. I see myself over there, far away, in the yellow years of time.

I was the woman of a man always wandering the face of the earth. He and I would take to the road, sacks on our backs, and head off to hunt for work. We ruined our feet, worked our fingers to the bone: hammering fences, branding animals, whatever came our way, whatever it was. No one was left in our town. Two, maybe three. And the church bell, mute, dead of thirst. Until one time, when the big drought came . . .

I'm boring you. Grandma's always telling the same story. Come on, let's put the beans on to soak. You can't sleep? I never sleep. My whole life practicing and I still don't know how. Sit by me, the kitchen's the best place. Grandma knows. For a night without sleep, for a day without soul, it's the best. The stove never goes out. Never.

Did I tell you about the moon people? The ones that came here. I didn't see them, no. They weren't to be seen, they weren't to be

touched. Moon people who came on heaven's toboggan. God's truth, by this cross. If you hear different, don't believe it. Here in the city, I know the rumor goes around. That human people have walked on the moon, but they're lying. When you don't know how to read, they mock you. But to climb up from here to there, think about it, who could do that? They, the moon people, traveled from there to here. That's different. It's downhill.

Friends of your grandfather's. Very gentlemanly with me. And with Grandpa, just as you're hearing: hand and glove. They didn't know anybody in the city. Neither did we. We'd come from another moon ourselves.

The desert. You never saw it. Nothing, no one. And the big drought came. With the last few drops we bathed the chicken, people say that brings rain. A lot of praying, a lot of candles. Nothing. So, goodbye, we're leaving to never return, with all our clothes on our backs. A trip through dead land, a pilgrimage of departees. Far, far, like never before. We crossed the Salgado River, dirty and shallow, and walked and walked toward the beyond, in search of green, against the sun's path by day, following the map of the stars by night. And at long last, it happened at night, the glow, the apparition: the train tracks. We reached the station more dead than alive. We put down our coins, bills wrinkled and old, what we saved and what we sold, all of it: two tickets to as far as we can go. And chuggachuggachuggachugga the train, toooot, tooooooooot, day and night, night and day, we stayed still and the world traveled, a different world, trees and pretty, clean houses galloping past.

And it stopped. It was over. They told us to get off. Outside it was raining, we entered the rain. Standing in the rain, the two of us. Our mouths open, our arms wide, rain that rained all God's tears.

And we entered the city. Us, like blind people caught in a shootout. Things never seen. People all bunched together, in a hurry. Automobiles in packs, howling like wild beasts. Machines chasing people, machines eating people. Everything forbidden. No corner to pee or sleep. Those who can read, read: "Forbidden." Those who can't, learn by blows, the poor man's school.

Yes, son, I know. The moon people, right. I take pleasure in parading the words, but I don't get lost.

I'll tell you. When the moon people arrived, no one knew. Grandpa was working, a pack animal in the bakery. He didn't speak to anyone. His back bent low under the firewood, under the bread, he brayed to himself. A burro without a tail? An ass of a burro. Gray skin, long hairy ears. And then, it happened. He cocked one ear, and the music entered him. The music of the moon people, playing for him. Believe me, like I'm telling you: the music deburroed him. Grandpa became a human being again, he was saved. The baker used to give us leftovers to eat. Not any more. A human being he didn't need.

Later, Grandpa kept on hearing the music. The moon people cured his leg. The cobra was inside his leg, big cobra, deep bite. It happened in the cane field, during the harvest, flying machete, far away. Old story, one that never ends. The wound closed up, all healed, and one day, whoosh, the cobra woke up, broke through the scabs, it smelled bad, it was rotting. And the music entered his leg, the music kicked out the cobra. On his new leg, Grandpa danced.

Dance, drink, eat. A great life. The moon people wanted to see everything. Let's go here, let's go there. Crazy about the city, real pleasure seekers. Grand fine places, white skins, golden hair, silver clothes, imagine it if you can. You'll never go there, never. Squat face, no poor allowed. The moon people could, wind that opens doors, and Grandpa behind and me on his arm, stepping like a queen, "At your service, señora." Money? None. The moon people played and there was no charge, no paying, let's have some music, let the party continue. They don't sleep, those moon people. Nighthawks, open eyes. Like you and me, in that way.

And one night, no more moon people, the party was over. They left. Where, who knows. No one was the knower of that secret. They're down there, I'd say, in the low heavens.

What were they like? Like little Martians, you mean, with antennas? You're not listening. The moon people couldn't be seen.

Time passed. Jobs, children, backbreaking work. I didn't know how to count the years, I couldn't tell you.

I know that one night Grandpa was asleep and I heard the sound. Just like that, all of a sudden. The music came out of his body. She came out of his pores, into the air, filled the darkness. I shook Grandpa, woke him up. What's wrong? No one understood.

No one knew. The music was still inside Grandpa. The moon people had left her with him. She was rather capricious, came out when she felt like it. Then his body would sing, it would light up, light that resounded in the air. She kept no fixed days or hours. As she came, so she went. It was a time of music, nights filled with playing, the entire barrio in the house, people from far away, crowds. We'd spend the whole night in the music and keep on going after dawn. You could see the music with your ears, she had colors. Whoever listened was reborn. Even the air was thankful, the birds kept quiet.

All the birds mute, while she was with us. She was better than they were and they knew it. They came in flocks, they cocked their ears.

It lasted as long as she wanted. And then, goodbye. She didn't come back. A lot of waiting for nothing. Never, never again. It was over, she had gone out. Poor world. Poor world without music.

Silence is beautiful. I like it. But that silence . . . Grandpa's hair went white, his black locks the color of milk. Look at this picture, see? Grandpa slept. He drank, he called to her, he slept. He broke everything, he picked fights, scattered bottles, then snored again.

That's what he died of. Drunk, calling to her, he died of music.

Go to sleep, go ahead.

Come on, come on, stay a while. Come up to the light, don't fall asleep on me. A small favor.

Grandma needs a letter. I've got a mailman. The neighbor on this side, you know him. He's very sick, really he's dying. Nice guy, he offered to take a letter to heaven for me. I thanked him, said no.

Grandpa in Paradise? He was no saint. Now I think: God has to know the address, he'll forward it.

I don't know my letters. I'm asking you, you go to school. Write it. I'll sign below, my scribble. Write to the one chosen by the moon. Hurry, the mailman's leaving.

Tell him:

> don't be sad,
> it doesn't matter that you're dead,
> just the same we're still entwined.

Tell him that tonight the music was here.

Window on the Word (VIII)

The woodsmen arrived, and the rabbi had nothing to offer them. So the rabbi went to the garden and spoke to it. He spoke to the plants with words that came from the damp earth, like them. And the plants received the words and suddenly matured and bore fruit and flowers. And thus the rabbi could tend to his guests.

The Cabala tells the story. And the Cabala says that the rabbi's son wanted to do it too, but the garden was deaf to his words and not one plant believed or grew.

The rabbi's son couldn't do it. But the rabbi? Could the rabbi repeat his own feat? The Cabala doesn't say. What would happen to the rabbi if neither the orange tree, nor the tomato plant, nor the jasmine tree answered him ever again?

Does the word know to fall silent when the moment that needs it has passed or the place that desires it has moved on? And the tongue, does it know how to die?

Story of One Day in the Café

Behind the counter, Prudencio leafs through the news. Without taking his eyes off the paper, he reaches up to the row of bottles and uncorks one.

"Nothing ever happens here," he grunts. He leaves the newspaper, serves me a glass of wine, and begins to fold paper napkins.

I sit at my table. From here, from the back, I can see the swinging door. It's not a day for a lot of bustle, but a few people seek the shade, wet their whistles, and go back out into the summer. Between customers, Prudencio grinds coffee, flicks a feather duster across the gallery of soccer and tango heroes, or stops to pat affectionately the X ray of his stomach. In a gold frame at the center of the portrait collection hangs the X ray: inside Prudencio's belly, like a radiant sun in a foggy scene, lies a shining bullet.

When he comes over to fill my empty glass, Prudencio starts telling, one more time, the story of that gunshot. In today's first edition, he's riding through the pass, whistling, minding his own business, when a man bent on revenge mistakes him for his twin brother, the cruelest bandit in the region, and shots ring out from the rocks. The horse falls on his belly. Prudencio tries to climb up the rockface, but slips. The first bullet sends his hat flying. More bullets rain down.

Batepapo saves me. Prudencio is at the climax of his tragedy when in walks Batepapo with his hat and his harlequin's outfit, twirling his colorful cane in one hand, holding a leash in the other. The leash doesn't lead a dog, but a lion.

Prudencio, who's already rolling down the ravine covered in blood, has no choice but to interrupt his agony. Opening his big owl's eyes and stretching wide his pelican's mouth, he declares: "No animals allowed."

You can't leave the lion at the door either, because it will scare away the customers.

The beast is left tied to a tree and Batepapo takes the table by the window. Prudencio brings him a drink, and while he taps the bottle with a spoon to shake up the beer, he praises the vanquished: the bird in its cage, the horse in its bridle, the sheep on the grill, the chicken in the frying pan, and the lion carpeting the living room.

Batepapo doesn't even look at him.

Batepapo, an artist of great fame, knows how to be a human cannon-ball, a trapeze artist without a net, and a clown who greets the multitudes by taking off his head, hat and all. But the arts of the tent don't have much of an audience anymore. The Great World Circus folded, and in the division of its assets, Batepapo got the lion. This morning he offered it to the city zoo. The veterinarians checked it over, and it was rejected: the lion has a hernia.

I listen to Batepapo tell of his misfortune while I admire, from the window, the serene majesty of the beast lying in the shade of the tree. From the lion's neck hangs a sign:

FOR SALE

The lion looks at me and yawns, showing off all his teeth, and I recall the flea Bambalina, who was an acrobat and lived in a matchbox. Bambalina, artist of the small circus. My friend Dudú, the insect trainer, would bring her to the café. Three times a day he let her bite him. Breakfast, lunch, and dinner.

Batepapo hasn't ever heard of that flea. He scratches his back with his cane to be polite, but he doesn't take his eyes off his lion for sale. It's obvious he couldn't care less about the subject.

How long has it been since old Dudú stopped coming to the café? No one has heard of him since.

At the table by the other window, the one that looks out on the train station, Doña Poca sips her sweet café con leche while the duel gets fought under the sun in the town where Prudencio used to live.

I can't hear very well because of the uproar at the center tables, but I know the story. Prudencio is fighting a duel for the sullied honor of his lady. The enemy shoots first. The bullet grazes him. Then Prudencio lowers his gun, shoots at the ground, and says nobly: "I forgive you." But it turns out that his rival, the scoundrel, has another bullet in his pistol.

"This one," says Prudencio, and between thumb and forefinger he holds up the projectile hanging from his keychain. Prudencio pulls up his shirt to show the scar across his belly. Doña Poca nods, her mouth open.

Then, while Prudencio goes off tray in hand, called by other duties, Doña Poca returns to hers. She watches the other side of the avenue. She spends her days seated at that table, her glasses always on, her eyes fixed on the iron grillwork of the station's main gate. The station has been dead for years, no train arrives, no train leaves. But Doña Poca waits.

"So, what's up?"

"I'm waiting."

"What are you waiting for, Doña Poca?"

And she shrugs her shoulders.

Hands folded, she waits. Perhaps she's waiting for her departed children, off in who knows what far-flung part of the world, or perhaps she's just waiting until her time on earth is done.

Don Tránsito has arrived. Ragged, shriveled, and dragging his feet, he goes from table to table taking bets.

Batepapo sings out his numbers, and here and there other people I don't know also make their bets. From my table I can hear Doña Poca argue, muttering about her troubles. And when my turn comes, Don Tránsito complains. He tells me he said to her: dreams don't lie, Doña Poca, and that's true, it's a proven fact, but it's not my fault, nor the dream's either. Doña Poca played 66, because she'd seen it clear as could be, but the winner was 88. Don Tránsito defends himself, says that she dreamt well, but saw poorly, and that's what she gets for sleeping without her glasses.

I bet, too. On 77, woman's legs, on 22, crazy woman, and on 20, fiesta. Dreams that chase me, numbers I follow. Some day they'll save me from poverty, I say, this mania of mine for dreaming and waiting must be good for something.

A fat man in uniform with a gun in his belt enters the café. Don Tránsito turns pale, but the arm of the law points at Batepapo: "Outside there's a lion parked illegally."

Batepapo gets up. Looking at the clock on the wall, he agrees: "You've come just in time, officer."

And he begs, "Please, help me chase the little animal away."

The two go outside.

A roar shakes the café.

I look out the window: the lion is licking his chops.

Batepapo comes back alone. He sits down and makes a face as if to say, that's life. There are so many members of the forces of order, no one will notice the absence of that one.

And thus, without anything noteworthy, from one trifle to another, time passes. The only light, a sickly lamp, pushes reluctantly at the invading shadows, while outside the sun is setting and the moon is rising. The voices fade and I no longer know what is said by the ones who speak, if they say anything at all. Prudencio's operatic voice takes over. For one of his last customers, Prudencio competes in the Olympics. The shot comes from some hidden corner of the stands, when he is about to be crowned world champion of the thousand-meter run. He falls, just short of the finish line, bathed in blood.

Prudencio gets up to go to the cash drawer. Batepapo, tired of waiting for buyers, pays his bill and goes off in the dusk, leading his lion by the leash. Doña Poquita also tires of waiting for her children or whomever. When she goes, she says: "It hurts." But she doesn't say what.

And no one comes. Only a wretched child, who ducks in the door and asks for something to take home for supper, says his belly sounds like a busy signal and he hasn't even a bit of chicken broth to quiet the noise.

I'm the last. I stay. I know it's a useless show, but I stay. I can see that today won't bring the woman who left me without fire or desire, nor will tomorrow bring a shaman or a dental surgeon who can pull her out of me with one tug and without anesthesia.

I get up, I get dizzy. I sit down, I stand up again.

I empty my pockets and manage to figure out that I can still pay for another bottle of wine and another pack of cigarettes.

Leaning on his elbows on the counter, Prudencio adds up the day's take. With a pencil behind his ear, he concludes: "You can't earn a thing here."

Prudencio raises his eyebrows, gives me a threatening look. It's evident that he plans to spring another of his heroic feats on me, to finish off the night by painting red the snows of Siberia or the sands of the Sahara. But I turn my back and he falls silent.

I drink. I smoke. I give thanks for the silence that resounds in the deserted café.

In the windows, night falls.

Between the empty tables magic shadows dance.

Window on Memory (III)

He who names, calls. And someone comes, without an appointment, without explanations, to the place where his name, said or thought, is calling him.

When this happens, one is justified in believing that no one ever completely leaves as long as the beckoning, reckoning word that brings him does not die.

Story of the Hunter

A man sits alone in a café. At his side, an empty chair. On the table, two glasses of wine. The man drinks from one, and toasts to the other.

Later, the metal security gate comes down and the man leaves with a bottle in his hand and vanishes amid the drifting automobiles, mumbling who knows what.

In the end he collapses against a wall and snores, with his bottle as a pillow.

A cat, sleeping under the still-warm motor of an automobile, dreams about a school of hake or a harem of Angoras.

And someone named El Gato sleeping in a doorway, dreams that a tremendous shot is flying toward the corner of his invincible net, and the crowd is already screaming "Goooooooool!" when his fingers miraculously deflect the white projectile, which gets lost in the clouds. El Gato turns over on the mattress of old newspapers, the unbeatable guardian of the three poles continues flying, traveling

toward glory, toward the World Cup, but he gets held up at the stations of time and arrives centuries late. At the stadium gates, a statue in livery wearing a periwig holds him back.

He awakes with the first light.

El Gato scares the cat, wraps a rag around his elbow, and breaks the window of the car. There's no radio hidden under the seat.

Then he leans on the drunk slumped against the wall. He explores his pockets. Empty.

A few blocks over, he lays a trap: he ties a wire around the base of a tree and pulls it tight across the sidewalk to a column, a hand's breadth from the ground.

Crouched down, he waits. Doña Poca, an old lady with glasses who isn't even carrying a purse, trips and falls flat. Doña Poca's glasses smash to bits on the sidewalk.

Despicable prey. El Gato shrugs his shoulders and leaves. Angrily, he kicks a Coca-Cola cap. A day that starts bad, gets worse.

He spends the time hanging out, wandering, looking for someone absentminded. And at dusk people in uniform corner him and almost catch him. He escapes by climbing impossible walls and slipping from shadow to shadow.

Later, he curls up in a hiding place.

A toy top spins and buzzes, a shimmering top to lift your sorrows. El Gato fixes his gaze on that little bit of vertigo and for a moment he forgets his whining belly and trembling bones.

He nibbles on a moist cracker that tastes as if it were made of gum. A dog sniffs and comes over; El Gato sends him away. In other times, El Gato had a dog. Not any more. That friend was blown away by a bullet meant for El Gato, and ever since he doesn't want anything to do with stray dogs that come up, seeking, like him, warmth and food.

To be alone doesn't hurt. El Gato is used to it. To feel lonely is something else. Sniffing glue, El Gato calls out to Saint George. Saint George is rough and hot-tempered, a womanizer, a trouble-maker. A surly saint, not even God can tell him what to do. He lives up there, like the clouds, and he comes when he feels like it. He comes down like the rain. The rain chases him out, it wets his lance.

Tonight he won't come. That was for sure.

But the next night, very late, El Gato awakes, aroused by the groaning of a motor approaching from afar, from up where the wind turns. And he sees a wisp of red smoke crossing the sky. The enemy of the dragon of misfortune is coming. Saint George appears in helmet and war feathers, lance in hand, astride a Yamaha motorcycle: El Gato leaps aboard and hangs on for the ride, hugging the iron armor of the warrior saint.

The winged motorcycle takes him hunting. Saint George's lance opens the way and they cross the city and traverse the night, traveling against the wind, on the way to their fate.

It's nearly dawn when they land in an unfamiliar plaza. El Gato stays, the saint departs.

The plaza, a vast ring of doorways, rises above the shining lights of the city that's awakening below. El Gato wanders aimlessly around the circle of columns. On this deserted hilltop, all the lights are out and all the doors are closed, have been for years or centuries. After walking a bit, El Gato discovers that someone is here.

He spies him from behind: a human bulk seated on a bench.

El Gato approaches, crouched low, an iron bar in his fist. But before El Gato strikes the blow, the bulk tilts to the side and falls.

Death scares El Gato; but not dead people, no. Death is not in dead people. She bites, eats, and leaves.

He looks at him up close, he pats him: a frozen gentleman with a well-trimmed mustache lying in his blood, the handle of a knife thrust out of his chest. The dead man's open eyes, big as eggs, ask why.

Up to now, El Gato had seen the kind of dead who leave the world without so much as a stick with which to defend themselves, or a handkerchief with which to console themselves, or a coin with which to pay for their sins. But this body is a Christmas present. It's got a diamond ring and a gold watch, and in its pockets a fat alligator-skin wallet.

What will he do with so much?

He'll break open the night, buying drinks for the whole city.

He'll buy himself a beach.

He'll rent the stadium one Sunday and the best players in the world will play for him in the empty stadium, him alone, seated on a chair in the middle of the presidential box, smoking a cigar.

He'll go into the most expensive restaurant, floor of mirrors, ceiling of crystal, and he'll order all the dishes on the menu.

On the balcony, open to the sun, the mayor is sweating buckets. Down below in roaring commotion is a sea of children in rags, a foam of hands raised toward the sky: dressed up like Santa Claus, the mayor throws down toys from above.

The toys rain down over the tumultuous crowd; poor children have a right to happiness too. These lucky kids dash and flail about, throwing punches and insults, stepping all over each other. A life-sized doll knocks over several; a space rocket strikes another right between the eyes; candies fall like rocks.

El Gato watches from a distance. He has a top and a secret.

At traffic lights, fast-talking children sell contraband cigarettes and little tubes of oxygen, just the thing for the lady's purse or the gentleman's pocket.

El Gato greets a couple of acquaintances and walks on, as cool as can be. "How are you doing?"

"Okay."

El Gato knows: if he divulges, he dies.

But he can't resist. A magical shop window is stronger than he, and in goes El Gato to buy an immense color television set, as big as the movies.

The radios, the TV, the newspapers proclaim: "After a sensational investigation, the police have captured the murderer of the businessman found dead by the gates of the Plaza of Silence. A minor, who has committed a number of misdemeanors, with no fixed address or . . ."

He has no name. Nor any age. Try and figure out what day he turned up in this mud hole. He says he was born on February 29, because he doesn't like birthdays.

With a number on his chest, El Gato confronts the black eye of the camera. The magnesium flash ignites, the shutter clicks.

Window on the City (I)

Under the archways of the plaza, a fakir has swallowed a number of spoons already and is now stuffing down a garden hose, while his women play flutes and tambourines, and a few people toss him coins.

Slumped in a corner, someone moves his fingers in the air. The fingers dance, as if playing the trumpet. From the invisible instrument a sad tune issues forth.

An old woman in rags calls out her magic potion against poverty, the best Christmas present, just a hundred, one hundred a bottle, he who buys is spared, he who denies despairs. No one listens to her. A thousand, just one thousand, announces a prophet of the Messiah's imminent visit, and the crowd shouts: "Je-sus!"

Next to the prophet roars a lion. Every time they pull his tail, he roars. A thousand, just one thousand, the prophet offers, come on over folks, the chosen will see him, they'll hear him, one thousand, come on over: "A loud round of applause, he's coming now! He's on his way down! He's nearly here!"

"Je-sus! Je-sus!" screams the plaza, and the roars of the lion accompany the cries and applause from people clapping their hands and craning their necks toward the heavens.

The heavens, hidden by exhaust from the motors, can't see the multitude watching it.

Story of the Second Visitation of Jesus

And down He comes. He arrives hanging from an open umbrella. An unexpected breeze keeps him floating for a good while above the crowd. Gripping the umbrella with both hands, the son of God can't keep the breeze from raising his gown and uncovering his human nudity.

Because of the breeze, he lands in the fountain. The devout, dumbfounded by the miracle, see him emerge from the waters amongst the marble angels.

Jesus shakes himself like a wet dog.

Batepapo, dressed in the clothes of a prophet, applauds. A pull on the tail and the lion roars. But the people watching the spectacle are motionless. Motionless and silent.

In the plaza, sanctuary of apparitions, the poor want to be rich
   and the rich want to be few,
    the blacks want to be white
   and the whites want to live forever,

the children want to be grownups

and the grownups want to be children,

the single want to be married

and the married want to be widowed.

"Inhabited inhabitants!" shouts Jesus. "Yesterday I will say what I'm saying now! You—we—are crazy!"

Everyone looks, cross-eyed with astonishment, at the dripping dishrag who waves his long arms like a windmill's sails and splashes them with water and asks strange questions: "Look at heaven. Will it give you Paradise or will it give you a stiff neck? Where is the kingdom, if not in the exile that seeks it?"

Batepapo applauds, a lone and indifferent clapping, and makes the lion roar. The son of God turns to the wild animal, its mouth still open, and pointing to it speaks to all as if they were one: "If the beast attacks you, what will you do? Will you pray? Will you resign yourself and let God's will be done? Or will you climb a tree? My dad doesn't like it when you use him as an alibi for cowardice or stupidity."

The lion looks at him, studies him. In the crowd, enemy rumors fly.

"This isn't the one," a señora murmurs, giving the beer-bellied and ragged Messiah a dirty look. "I saw Jesus on TV and he looked just like Burt Lancaster."

"Exile is within you, and the kingdom as well!" insists the Lord's messenger, but the murmurs grow and the first shouts can be heard: "Let him bleed! Let him prove he's God! Let him bleed from his side!"

Impassive, Jesus continues: "The eye that can't be seen is the eye that sees."

"I don't see anything," mutters Doña Poca, who got caught up in the hubbub while walking, groping toward her watchtower in the café.

Crushed by the crowd, the vendors elbow their way through and cry out their merchandise—"peanuts, peeeeeeanuts, peanut-maaaaaan, fresh hot churros, ice creeeeeam"—while distrust turns to fury against the rotund redeemer, who wears no more jewelry than a lump on his bald head and who doesn't give away splinters from the

holy cross, or thorns from the crown, or anything at all. A bombard-
ment of outcries: "Let him bleed! Let him bleed!"

"Let him eat a live cockroach!"

"Impostor!"

"Give us back our money!"

But then an argument breaks out in the middle of the crowd,
diverting for a moment the course of their anger: some maintain that
the real Jesus was killed by the Italians and others insist it was the
Jews. Some swear that he was resurrected on Holy Saturday and others know that it happened on Sunday morning at ten o'clock sharp.

Jesus seizes the ephemeral truce and gives their rage the slip.

He's standing, straight and tall on the rocks, facing the sea that wets him with spray. On his shoulder a sea gull sleeps. I approach from behind. He doesn't move and neither does the gull.

Then he sits on a rock and hangs his head between his knees. I think he's complaining: "They hate me because they think they owe me favors."

I sit at his side. He raises his head and faces the wind.

"We never learn from experience," he says without looking at me. "Father forbade me to come back."

He scratches his scraggly beard: "He doesn't love them, because they're almost good. Neither does the Devil, because they're almost bad."

Jesus looks so much like my lost friend, the flea trainer, that I almost say: "Dudú."

And I think that my country is a handkerchief, a folded handkerchief. But he looks at me, and his eyes reflect a scene that's not of this world, the sparkle of a limitless place that not even the sun knows.

"Soon I'll be thirty-three," he says.

The sleeping gull flies off and is lost in the sky.

"They'll listen to me after I die," he says. "Here on earth, that's the way it is."

He picks up a handful of sand, lets it fall bit by bit.

We return to the plaza. There are a few people, each one caught up in his own comings and goings, but no one pays us the slightest heed.

"They wanted me to jump without an umbrella," Jesus sighs, by the fountain. "A pancake from God."

And he smiles sadly for the picture. We pose together under a palm tree. The photographer, hooded under his box camera, pulls the shutter with a little string. Then he carries out a few mysterious operations in the darkness, pulls out the negative, dries it in the air, and sticks his head under the hood again.

When the picture comes out of the bucket of water and arrives, at last, in my hands, I discover that I'm alone. In the picture no one appears at my side. No one, except for the palm tree.

Window on Punishment

It was Christmas, and a Swiss man gave a Swiss watch to his Swiss son.

The child took the watch apart on his bed. And he was playing with the hands, the spring, the crystal, the winder, and all the little gears, when his father found him and gave him a terrible beating.

Until then, Nicole Rouan and her brother had been enemies. From that Christmas on—the first Christmas she remembers—the two of them were friends for life. On that day, Nicole learned that she too would be punished in all the years to come, because instead of asking the clocks of the world what time it was, she would ask them what they were like inside.

Story of Another Day in the Café

Batepapo comes in without his cane.

He smokes with a cigarette holder, drinks French cognac. No longer does he wear the clothes of a clown or a prophet. For a while now he has been wearing an impeccable white suit, matching shoes, and a tie with a gold clip.

The lion is busy, far from here. Batepapo no longer has him for sale: now he rents him out. The idea occurred to him when a down-and-dirty hoodlum came to hire the beast to punish an unfaithful girlfriend. Since then, Batepapo has been solving the domestic problems of marriages in crisis and oversize families.

Jesus, or Dudú, or whatever his name was, was never heard from again, nor did I dare ask. I imagine he's in one of God's resting places. The truth is that one or two little pieces of advice wouldn't have done me any harm, but there was no time.

That's what I get for being quiet. If words were fattening, I'd be too big for this world, given all the ones I've swallowed. I work at

whatever comes along, whatever turns up, always with my mouth shut, and I spend the rest of my time the same way, here in the café, days without humor, nights without joy, and that's how I live. Footprints in the water.

Today Prudencio tells me he used to be a diamond smuggler. There he is, crossing the jungle when he comes upon the most beautiful woman in the world, naked in the river, and for having seen her he is doomed. The father of the beauty, a dwarf with three legs, a reptile's body, and a barbed tail, shoots him in the belly.

I think I'm starting to believe him.

The rain pelts against the windows of the café.

This afternoon the air has a rare something. Smoke, and not just from cigarettes, floats in the air and yellows the dark atmosphere and Doña Poca's ancient parchment skin.

Seated at the next table, I share her window. Today I see her up close. She is dressed like never before, black silk and threadbare lace dredged up from the depths of some old trunk, and permeated by the perfume from a sprig of violets in her buttonhole. Through new glasses, Doña Poca contemplates the rain beating on the gates of the dead station.

The señora does not come from the station: she doesn't enter so much as appear, like an emanation from the smoke or the rain.

She sits at Doña Poca's table, leans forward, squeezes the old woman's hands. She has ash-colored hair and like Doña Poca is small and skinny. I hear her whisper, or I think I hear: "I'm here."

Doña Poca, perplexed, pulls her hands away and asks: "Are you retired too?"

The new arrival moves her head slowly, murmurs: "It's been years, but I'm here."

"We retired women get very poor treatment," Doña Poca mumbles.

The woman speaks, her voice like a thread: "Now you're not alone," she says.

And Doña Poca: "Do you have children? I have a daughter, one left. She lives far from here."

And pointing to the station, as if imparting a confidence, she says: "She'll come, today or tomorrow."

That woman turns her head and I meet her gaze. She lowers her eyes.

Window on the City (II)

I'm alone in a foreign city, and I don't know anyone, nor do I understand the language. But suddenly someone shines in the middle of the crowd, shining suddenly like a word lost on the page or any patch of grass on the skin of the earth.

Story of the Other

You make breakfast, like you do every day.

Like every day, you take your son to school.

Like every day.

Then, you see him. You see him on the corner, reflected in a puddle on the sidewalk. And you nearly get run over by a truck.

Then, you go off to work. And you see him once more, in the window of a gin-mill, and you see him in the crowd that the subway devours and vomits back onto the street.

At dusk, your husband picks you up. And on the way home, just the two of you, quietly breathing the poison of the air, you see him again in the whirlwind of the streets: that body, that wordless face that asks and calls.

And from then on you see him with your eyes open, no matter where you look, and you see him with your eyes closed, no matter what you think. And with your eyes you touch him.

That man comes from a place that is not this place and from a time that is not this time. You, mother of, wife of, are the only one who sees him, the only one who can. You no longer hunger for anyone, hunger for anything, but every time he appears and vanishes, you feel an irrepressible need to laugh and sob the laughs and sobs you've been swallowing all your life, dangerous laughs, forbidden sobs, secrets hidden in who knows what corner of your insides.

And when night falls, while your husband sleeps, you turn your back and dream that you awaken.

Window on the Nape of the Neck

Things are the owners of the owners of things and I can't find my face in the mirror. I speak what I don't say. I am but I'm not. And I take a train to where I'm not going, in a country exiled from me.

Window on the Face

A stupid machine?

A letter that has no return address and is delivered to the wrong destination?

A stray bullet, that some god shot by mistake?

We come from an egg much smaller than the head of a pin, and we live on a rock that spins around a dwarf star into which it will some day crash.

But we're made of light, as well as carbon and oxygen and shit and death and so much else. And after all, we've been here ever since the beauty of the universe needed someone to see it.

Story of the Wandering Girl Who Traveled into the River and up the Night

She was always going. But she'd return. Several times they gave her up for drowned. But she came back.

The family wanted to educate her: "Breathe, Garúa," they'd tell her. "Pay attention to your teacher, she knows."

And they'd tell her: "Breathing is one thing that does you a lot of good."

Given air and water, she preferred water. And there was no way to get her to mend her ways. At dusk she would plunge into the Olimar River, and in its depths she would let herself be and let herself flow. The moon opened a path in the watery night and the polished stones of the river were stars in a reverse sky: Garúa would see them pass, and see the fish pass, and the arms of the plants waving, and in that luminous darkness no one could find her and she owed obedience to no one.

In the wetness, Garúa lived. In the dryness, no. In the dryness, she wanted to sleep. Sleep was the only thing she wanted. Lying under the covers, she'd dream that she was galloping on the back of a swordfish that turned into a shark that turned into a whale that was an island that broke off from the world. And on board the island Garúa navigated the waves of the sky.

And it happened. But not like that. The truth came out by the fire.

On cold nights, men in ponchos curl up by the fire. In circles of maté and cane liquor, they smoke and tell lies that tell the truth. That's how they come in from the cold and from the foolishness of living, and that's how they spend the time that the day gathered for the night to fritter away.

Garúa was a topic by the fire. Some detested the tomboy who never tied up her hair or asked for a doll. Others were curious about the little mermaid, and some admired the Amazon of the water.

By the fire it was said that Garúa hunted ducks by their feet. She hunted them in the lake, from under water. Submerged, without raising her head, Garúa would tie the ducks' legs with a long thread. When she had caught a good number, she'd give a yank from below and swim them to shore. Once there, they were ready for plucking.

Until one day, it was said by the fire, a duck she had just tied took fright and took flight and the entire flock flew after him, and after the ducks flew Garúa, hanging by the thread.

By the fire it was said that her mother saw her pass by, hugging the tail of that great comet of ducks climbing high into the sky. And watched until she was lost in the heavens.

Garúa passed the bird who sang out his own name and she could recognize it despite the uproar of the fleeing ducks. And she went on climbing, and flew over the rivers drawn on the school map, and from up there she saw the back of the purple eagle and beyond that she saw that the earth had red flesh and green skin and blue veins.

And Garúa, hanging onto the ducks, went into the distance. Everything sounded more and more remote and everything grew smaller, until the voices of the world went out and the world was wrapped in clouds. Garúa gripped the thread with all her strength and entered a white silence where all she heard was the flapping of the flying ducks, while the clouds swam by silently, serenely.

The arrow of ducks crossed the cotton sea of cloud and then the heavens opened and Garúa rose through the colors, from sky-blue to violet, and she entered the night and flew up through the night toward the moon.

Traveling toward the moon, Garúa passed the wandering star, the one that searches for the lost road to earth,

and she saw the warrior of the desert, using his rifle as a walking stick, climbing,

and she saw the bolt of lightning that exploded to answer the corn's thirst

and she saw the Great Dog on his throne, surrounded by a court of winged puppies,

and she saw the rainbow breaking open the night

and she saw the woman flying with vulture's wings

and she saw the keys to heaven's kingdom fall

and she saw the archangel dangling from a rope

and she saw Saint George riding his motorcycle down, lance at the ready,

and she saw Jesus hanging from an open umbrella.

She didn't see the invisible moon people traveling toward the world by toboggan, but she saw the moon. The moon, who sends the world music and lunacy. The moon, who transfigures dolphins and guides the wanderings of children along the bottoms of rivers.

Window on Utopia

She's on the horizon, says Fernando Birri. I go two steps closer, she moves two steps away. I walk ten steps and the horizon runs ten steps ahead. No matter how much I walk, I'll never reach her. What good is utopia? That's what: it's good for walking.

Window on Memory (IV)

Under the sea travels the song of the whales, calling to each other.

Through the air travels the whistle of the wanderer, who seeks a roof and a woman for the night.

And throughout the world and throughout the years travels Grandma.

Grandma travels by asking: "How much longer?"

She lets herself go from the roof of her house and floats above the earth. Her old ship travels toward childhood and being born and before: "How much longer until we arrive?"

Grandma Raquel is blind, but while she travels she sees bygone times, she sees the lost fields. There where the hens lay ostrich eggs, tomatoes are like pumpkins, and all clovers have four leaves.

Seated in her chair, well groomed and washed and powdered as can be, Grandma travels her return trip and invites us all along: "Don't be afraid," she says. "I'm not afraid."

And the slight boat slides through earth and time.

"A lot longer?" Grandma asks, while she goes.

Window on Memory (V)

The light of dead stars travels, and by the flight of their splendor they look alive.

The guitar, which does not forget its companion, makes music without any hand.

The voice travels on, leaving the mouth behind.